THE DOCTOR'S VALENTINE DARE

BY
CINDY KIRK

MILLS
BOON

First Published in Great Britain 2016
By Mills & Boon, an imprint of HarperCollins*Publishers*
1 London Bridge Street, London, SE1 9GF

© 2016 Cynthia Rutledge

ISBN: 978-0-263-91964-6

23-0216

Printed and bound in Spain
by CPI, Barcelona

From the time she was a little girl, **Cindy Kirk** thought everyone made up different endings to books, movies and television shows. Instead of counting sheep at night, she made up stories. She's now had over forty novels published. She enjoys writing emotionally satisfying stories with a little faith and humour tossed in. She encourages readers to connect with her on Facebook and Twitter, @cindykirkauthor, and via her website, www.cindykirk.com.

To my dear friend Anita Evans,
who reads all my books and always has
a kind word to say. Who knew when we began
working together all those years ago that we
would become lifelong friends? Thanks for
all your support. It means so much to me.

Chapter One

"I don't even know you." Josie Campbell gazed up at the tall, broad-shouldered man in bewilderment. "Why would I agree to go out with you?"

"How else can you get to know me?" Noah Anson shot her a charming smile showing a mouthful of straight white teeth. With jet-black hair, a just-short-of-olive skin tone and bright blue eyes, the effect was mesmerizing. Toss in the cashmere topcoat, dark hand-tailored suit and red Hermès tie, and, well, it was quite a tempting package.

From his confident demeanor, Josie surmised the man's past efforts to pick up women had met with great success.

Tempting for most women, Josie reminded herself. Not for her, because of several reasons, including the most obvious. "You're a stranger."

"I introduced myself." Noah spoke with barely suppressed impatience. He gestured with his head toward the counter. "If you require a personal reference, Cole will vouch for me."

Cole Lassiter, owner of the Hill of Beans coffee empire, stood behind the counter. At the moment, the successful entrepreneur was busy instructing one of his staff.

Josie didn't need a reference. Once Noah introduced himself, she'd recognized the name. He was the neurosurgeon who'd joined her father's medical practice last year.

Though she'd been back in Jackson Hole for over a month, this was the first time their paths had crossed.

Just recalling how he'd introduced himself made her smile. *Doctor* Noah Anson. He'd obviously added the doctor bit hoping to impress her. What he didn't realize was he'd have had a better chance by leaving it off. In her experience, physicians didn't make good boyfriends or relatives.

"Thank you for the dinner invitation." She offered a perfunctory smile and tried to ignore her reaction to the testosterone wafting off him in waves. "But I'm not interested."

Josie offered no further explanation. She'd learned years ago that having a valid reason often made no difference to a man convinced his way was the right way, the only way.

Noah's eyes, as blue as the Wyoming sky, sharpened. She swore she could hear the gears in that analytical mind of his whirring.

Finally, he nodded. "Understood."

Josie was surprised by the easy acquiescence. She'd gotten the distinct impression Noah was cut from the same bolt of cloth as her arrogant father and brothers. She'd expected him to redouble his efforts and turn on the charm. Or, at the very least, press for an explanation.

Feeling oddly disappointed, Josie turned toward the door. "Have a good day, Dr. Anson."

Before she could take a step, the latte was lifted from her hand. "Not so quickly."

Josie whirled and found herself staring into those vivid blue eyes. Eyes that now held a hint of amusement.

She suppressed a sigh and forced a stern expression. "Give me back my drink."

Actually, it wasn't her drink at all. She still held her own caramel macchiato. Noah had grabbed her employer's nonfat latte.

"There's an open table by the window. I'm not through making my case." Without waiting for a response the doctor crossed the crowded shop with long purposeful strides, Pauline's latte in hand.

Josie shot a frustrated glance in Cole Lassiter's direction. The man who, up to now, she'd considered a friend, merely lifted his shoulders. He appeared to be hiding a smile.

There was no reason she couldn't simply order another drink and stroll out the door without a backward glance. An option certainly, though a rather cowardly one. And, other than running away from her family all those years ago, Josie had never been a coward.

Heaving a resigned sigh, she followed Dr. Anson across the small dining area.

Though dressed for the wintery weather in a red plaid coat, jeans and clunky winter boots, she sat in the chair he pulled out with a fluid grace born of years of yoga. She placed her drink on the table, then began unbuttoning her coat. "You're going to buy me another latte. And within the next five minutes or I'll be late for work."

Noah grinned. "Of course."

Her gaze met his. Time seemed to stretch and extend. He really did have a nice smile. Too bad it was wasted on her. Knowing he was associated with her father made her tread carefully.

"Dr. Anson, I'm sure you're a perfectly likeable man. But I'm not interested in dating anyone at this time." Josie lifted the macchiato to her lips and a rebellious streak that had been the bane of her father's existence had her adding, "If you're interested in meeting someone new, may I suggest the produce aisle at the grocery store on the highway? Word is, that's a prime place in Jackson Hole for singles to connect."

Though the smile remained on his lips, his voice took on a clip of annoyance. "I don't have to prowl the aisles of a food market to find a date."

"Of course you don't," she said with a cheeky grin. "You prefer coffee shops."

To her surprise he laughed, a pleasant rumbling sound. Yet, when she started to rise, he reached out and grabbed her hand.

In the second it took Josie to jerk her fingers back, heat shot up her arm.

"You said five minutes." His sexy, deep voice held a hint of the East Coast…and a challenge. "More than enough time to change your mind."

Intrigued despite herself, Josie chuckled. "Arrogant much?"

"Confident. There's a difference." Noah took a sip of the nonfat latte and grimaced. "I have a proposition for you."

Those blue eyes focused on her again, sending a shiver through her body. If he wasn't a doctor, wasn't in practice with her father, wasn't—

Josie shoved the wistful thoughts aside. Hadn't she learned long ago that wishing things were different, wishing people were different, didn't change reality?

"First you ask me for a date. Now you have a proposition." She settled back in her seat and kept her tone light. "This just gets better and better."

"And this—" Noah shoved the nonfat latte aside and motioned to Cole for some coffee "—just gets worse and worse."

His disgust with the drink made her smile.

"It's not a proposition in the way you think." He spoke in a low tone, his gaze fixed on hers. "I'll explain."

Hoping she didn't regret the decision, Josie pulled the phone from her pocket and checked the timer. "Four minutes left."

His dark brows drew together in puzzlement.

"I can't be late for work."

"Tell Pauline you were with me." Noah waved a dismissive hand. "She'll understand."

Now it was Josie's turn to be confused. "You know my employer?"

"Pauline Bettinger is my grandmother."

Two weeks ago, Josie had not only accepted a part-time position as the wealthy widow's personal assistant, she'd taken a room in the woman's gorgeous home. While Josie knew that Daffodil Prentiss, a local hairstylist, was related to Pauline, she couldn't recall Noah's name ever being mentioned. "Does that mean you and Daffy are related?"

"Daffodil is my sister."

With long straight blond hair and an ethereal quality reminiscent of a flower child from the 1960s, Daffodil could not have been more different from her brother. The hairstylist had arrived in Jackson Hole during the years Josie had been away. "I don't believe I've ever seen you with Daffy."

Noah's expression remained guarded, his blue eyes intense. "We're estranged."

"I'm sorry to hear that." Josie's sympathy was sincere.

She knew all about dysfunctional family dynamics and the pain of estrangement. That was why she'd come home to heal her relationship with her father and oldest brother.

"I'm determined to bridge the gap between us." Noah's jaw lifted in a determined tilt. "To do that, I require your assistance."

Something in Noah's eyes told her, regardless of the reason for the rift, the wall that existed between him and his sister brought him great pain. Josie steeled her heart at the tug it produced. "I make it a point not to get involved in family matters."

"All I'm asking is you vouch for me. I'm hoping if you plead my case that might make a difference."

Josie didn't bother to hide her confusion. "I don't even know you."

"Exactly."

Before she could ask for clarification, a young high school girl brought his coffee. Noah slipped the girl a twenty and told her to keep the change. The teen's wide smile and effusive thanks made Josie give Noah the benefit of the doubt. Generosity wasn't something that could be learned.

Her heart softened, but not enough to reconsider. She began to rise. "Well, I need to—"

Noah put a restraining hand on her arm. "I still have two minutes."

A quick glance at the phone's screen confirmed that fact. Resigned, Josie sat back down.

"Five dates." Noah paused for a sip of coffee before continuing. "That should be enough time for you to get to know me. That way, when you plead my case with Daffy, you'll feel confident I only have her best interests at heart."

Though Josie knew this man's family problems were none of her concern, she liked Pauline and Daffodil. And she was sympathetic to anyone who wanted to mend broken family ties. After all, wasn't that the reason she'd returned to Jackson Hole?

"Why don't you have your grandmother put in a good word for you?" Josie had seen firsthand how close the two women were and knew Daffodil respected her grandmother's opinion.

"Gram attempted to mediate but her efforts caused a slight rift between her and Daffy that's only recently mended. I won't put her in the middle again." A muscle in his jaw jumped. "Daffy—well, let's just say she needs Gram to be on her side."

"Even if that means Pauline can't be on yours?"

"Yes."

Her heart flip-flopped as she realized she and Noah had something in common. He was as much an outsider looking in as she was in her family.

She brought the cup to her lips and took a thoughtful sip. "I'd be willing to mention to Daffodil that I ran into you and you seemed nice."

He shook his head.

"I promise to leave off the part about you stealing Pauline's drink." A smile tugged at her lips as she strove to lighten the mood.

His expression remained somber. "Daf would say you don't know me. She'd be right. At this point, you and I are strangers."

The misery in his eyes pulled at Josie. She had to resist the urge to reach over and give his hand a squeeze. "I hope you and Daffy resolve your differences, I truly do."

"But you won't help me." His voice turned as flat as his eyes.

Though she told herself he didn't deserve an explanation for her refusal, she felt as if she owed him *something*.

"It's just I have enough family issues of my own." Josie's voice grew thick and she cleared her throat. "I simply can't get in the middle of yours."

Josie thought of Noah often over the next few days. She couldn't stop thinking how he'd looked at her as if she was the only woman in the world.

She'd spoken with Pauline about the encounter with her grandson and his unusual request. A sadness had filled the older woman's eyes as she'd confirmed the estrangement between her two grandchildren.

Pauline had surprised her by adding, "In her own way, Daffodil is as mule-headed as her brother."

When Josie informed her employer she turned down Noah's odd request, Pauline had nodded and said that was her choice. Josie was left with the uneasy feeling her employer wished she'd agreed.

They hadn't spoken of the matter since that day. Pauline kept Josie busy with errands, correspondence and dress fittings. A prominent member of the hospital board, Pauline had been invited to attend a New Year's Eve masquerade ball thrown by Dr. Travis Fisher and his wife, Mary Karen, and was eager to look her best.

The couple's parties were well known. According to Pauline, the Fishers normally preferred casual events but this year they'd decided to go formal. Pauline insisted Josie attend as her plus one.

Josie felt a stir of excitement as the home in the mountains overlooking Jackson came into view. The large two-story house was lit up as bright as the sky on the Fourth of July. Silver glittery lanterns lined the walkway. The home's front door had been festively decorated with black-and-white tulle and two silver masks.

Though limited parking required most attendees to park

a good distance away on the side of the mountain road, Travis had hired several town cars to ferry the elegantly dressed partygoers from their vehicles to the front door.

As the sleek black vehicle approached the house, Josie saw men in tuxedoes and women in cocktail-length dresses and long gowns, all wearing masks, streaming through the front doors.

Seated next to her in the toasty warm town car, Pauline cast an admiring glance at the royal blue cocktail-length satin dress visible beneath Josie's fur coat. "I know I said it before, but you look very lovely this evening, my dear. Your mask is…incredible."

Her father, Dr. John Campbell, had given in to Josie's pleas and bought her the mask on a family vacation in Venice. The trip had been a halcyon time before his— and her brothers'—expectations of her had become too much to bear.

Josie raised her fingers and touched the papier-mâché edge. Multicolored in vivid shades with a gold leaf finish, the mask was anchored to her face with ribbons the same color as her dress.

Pauline's own mask was equally stunning. It had a silver leaf finish and was decorated with crackle glaze, macramé and Swarovski crystals. Her employer looked positively regal in a charcoal-colored gown that was the perfect foil for her silver hair pulled up in a stylish chignon.

"We're going to be the prettiest girls there," Josie declared and made Pauline laugh.

The two women entered the house arm-in-arm. After being greeted by their hostess, Pauline startled Josie by announcing she would meet her back in the foyer at twelve-thirty. According to her employer, mingling on their own would ensure they'd have much to talk about on their way home.

It seemed odd to Josie that the woman had asked her to come as her plus one, only to separate the instant they entered the home. Thankfully, Josie was comfortable being on her own. She'd had plenty of experience. For the past seven years she'd had only herself to rely on.

With head held high, she made her way through the spacious home, confiscating a glass of champagne from a passing waiter and a canapé from another. She gazed in open admiration at the black, white and silver balloons caught up in a shimmery net overhead, waiting to be dropped at midnight.

The great room at the back of the house brimmed with beautiful people of all ages and shapes, each wearing the requisite mask. As Josie wove her way through the crowd, her confidence received a boost when she became aware of several admiring glances being cast her way.

It might sound vain, but she knew she looked her best this evening. Although Josie hadn't been able to banish all the curl from her blond hair, tonight the strands hung in loose waves down her back. Not an out-of-control corkscrew in sight. Her strapless blue dress flattered her figure and fair complexion. Three-inch heels made her legs look longer than they were and brought her height up to five feet seven inches.

Despite knowing her eyes would remain hidden behind the mask for most of the evening, Josie had taken extra time with her makeup. Hoping to do justice to the green eyes that were said to be her best feature, she'd applied a smoky silvery sheen of shadow and several coats of mascara with a heavy hand.

A burst of laughter drew her gaze. Josie's red-painted lips curved upward at the sight of several couples engaged in conversation with a sandy-haired man she recognized as their host, Travis Fisher. He'd been busy attaching something to a black and white feather chandelier—obviously brought in for the occasion—when she and Pauline arrived.

Instead of standing in a quiet corner and sipping champagne, the proper thing for Josie to do would be to walk over and introduce herself.

She blamed her hesitation on the fact that this New Year's Eve gala was far different from the parties she attended in Portland. In those years away, Josie had discovered she preferred smaller, more intimate gatherings. In fact, it had become a tradition for her to usher in the New Year with friends, fondue and kirsch-wine cocktails.

Knowing the time had come to heal the rift in her family hadn't made leaving her friends and the life she'd built in Oregon any easier.

Of course, nothing said she couldn't return one day. Yet when her gaze had once again lingered on the majestic Tetons, she accepted that this rugged country was her home and she was here to stay.

The party tonight was an opportunity to reconnect with old friends and meet new ones. But first she had to assuage her curiosity. When she asked Mary Karen what her husband had been hanging on the chandelier, the pretty blonde simply smiled and encouraged her to check it out herself.

Josie stepped closer and narrowed her gaze. A sprig of dark green leaves and berries hung from a dark feather directly above her.

Was that, could that be, *mistletoe*?

"Gram said I'd find you here," a familiar masculine voice pronounced. "I'm happy you reconsidered."

Josie whirled.

Brilliant blue eyes behind a dark mask was all she saw before Noah's mouth closed over hers.

Chapter Two

Josie hadn't attained the age of twenty-nine without being kissed. In fact her first kiss had come at the tender age of fourteen by the fifteen-year-old neighbor boy. But never had she been kissed like this.

It started slowly, a gentle melding of lips. Noah's mouth was warm and inviting. Before Josie realized what she was doing, she'd stepped into him, winding her arms around his neck.

The instant his tongue pressed for entry, she opened her mouth. Fireworks exploded and her blood turned to fire. Suddenly, close wasn't close enough. She wanted, no, needed, more, needed to be under his skin.

As she pressed against his body, hers soft where his was rock-hard, she heard him mutter a curse. She'd just slid her fingers into his hair when he took a step back.

"Too many people." His gravelly voice seemed to come from far away. "We've got to slow this down."

Get yourself under control.

Though he didn't speak the words, she'd heard them all her life.

Even as Josie's heart continued to slam against her ribs, she managed a careless shrug, grateful for the mask concealing her heated cheeks.

"I've always enjoyed mistletoe." She gave a carefree laugh. "Perhaps a little too much."

The flicker in Noah's eyes told Josie he'd caught her meaning. She was saying she'd have enjoyed *any* kiss under a sprig of berries and leaves.

As if to illustrate, Josie grabbed the hand of a man who was strolling past. Thick chestnut hair tumbled above a half mask of red and gold. When he inclined his head questioningly, she pointed upward.

Something about the quick flash of his grin was vaguely familiar. The stranger didn't hesitate. He leaned close and placed his mouth against hers. Unlike her experience with the sharp-eyed doctor who stood watching, this lip-lock didn't ignite even the tiniest of sparks. Of course, that could simply be because all the fireworks had been used up moments before.

Josie stepped back and offered the stranger a smile. "Have a nice evening. Happy New Year."

"I'll definitely be seeing you around." Though his voice was slightly familiar, Josie didn't care enough to try to place him. She'd made her point.

"You don't have a clue who he is." Noah's voice sounded in her ear. Though he'd kept his distance while the kiss was in progress, he stepped forward the instant the other guy walked off.

Josie lifted one shoulder in a noncommittal shrug. "Does it matter?"

"He could have been your brother." Noah took her arm and steered her out of range of the mistletoe.

Josie stiffened, then chided herself for being so gullible. "Benedict is a good three inches taller."

"You weren't thinking about that when you jumped the guy," Noah pointed out.

"I didn't jump—" she began, then stopped when she saw the twinkle in the neurosurgeon's eyes. "Har. Har."

"I'd have laughed if it *had* been Benedict." Noah adroitly snagged two glasses of champagne from a passing waiter. "Even better…your father."

Josie's gagging noise made him chuckle.

She took a sip of champagne and gazed at him through lowered lashes. With broad shoulders, long legs and a lean athletic build, the man was made for black tie. The shiny dark strands of his hair, cut a bit too short for her taste, glistened like burnished walnut in the light of the chandelier.

The fingers wrapped around his own glass of champagne were long and elegant, much like an artist's. Then again, she supposed Noah was an artist of sorts. Instead of a garret, his studio was a brilliantly lit operating room and his brush, a scalpel.

The reminder that she'd kissed a doctor with such unrestrained passion had her wrinkling her nose.

"Is something wrong with your champagne?" He glanced around as if searching for a waiter.

"It's not the drink, it's you," she blurted then waited for the disapproving look.

Instead, Noah contemplated her as if she was a puzzle he was having difficulty solving.

"You're a doctor," she added for clarification, then flushed. Perhaps her father had been on to something with all his "think first" admonishments.

"Not for tonight," he said smoothly, taking her arm and moving them in the direction of the back of the house. "Tonight let me be simply the man in the black mask, who you enjoy kissing."

"I do not, ah, did not—"

One look from those brilliant blue eyes stopped the protest. She couldn't deny the explosive chemistry between them, any more than she could control the shivers his touch elicited.

"Are you suggesting we pretend to be someone we're not for the evening?" Though she found the thought intriguing, Josie knew she must have misunderstood. There was no way this straitlaced, serious doctor would suggest something so daring.

An emotion she couldn't quite decipher flickered in the depths of those amazing blue eyes. "Interested?"

Josie sipped her champagne and tried to figure out what was really going on here...

"Are you here with someone?" His tone turned brusque. "Is that the reason you're hesitating?"

"Actually." Josie placed a finger against lips that still tingled from his kiss. "I'm trying to decide who—or what—I want to pretend to be."

The fingers wrapped around her arm relaxed. He lifted the champagne flute with his other hand and took a sip. "You have any thoughts?"

"Let's play pirates," she suggested with a cheeky smile.

He choked on his champagne.

She merely smiled and waited for him to quit sputtering.

"Are you serious?"

"Totally."

He rubbed his chin. While he pondered the suggestion— likely creating a pro-con spreadsheet in his head—she glanced around the room.

Josie assumed most of those in attendance knew the

person behind each mask. It wasn't that easy for her. She'd been away too long.

Until she'd run across Noah, she might as well have been playing blind man's bluff. She still didn't understand why her employer insisted they go solo. Unless...

Could her running into Noah have been part of a plan? Pauline had certainly made it clear she'd like it if Josie helped him. "Did your grandmother know you were coming tonight?"

His brows pulled together in puzzlement. "I don't think so. Maybe. Why?"

"No reason." She relaxed and waved a hand. "Back to the original question. Do you want to play pirates?"

"There are so many ways to answer your question. Are we talking pillaging and plundering or do you expect me to talk like a pirate? Say things like ahoy and matey?"

The look of horror on his face made her grin. "Yer correct."

Okay, so maybe her own pirate accent was even worse than his, but Josie was already having fun.

Noah's obvious reticence made the playacting even more enticing. The remainder of the evening suddenly took on a glossy sheen, like the pages of a magazine she couldn't wait to devour.

Still, Noah resisted giving his agreement.

Shoving aside the thought that this man was just like her father and therefore someone to be given a wide berth, Josie extended her hand. "Don't be an ol' chumbucket, Cap'n. Put yer hand here and shake on the deal."

Noah stared at the dainty hand with the pink nails. Just when he thought the evening couldn't get any stranger, it did.

He took her hand. The feel of her skin against his put

all sorts of thoughts in his head. Actually, the thoughts had been there since he'd first seen her tonight.

The vivid blue cocktail dress had drawn his gaze to her breasts and the legs that appeared to go on forever. Certain parts of his anatomy had immediately sprung to life.

When his lips joined hers under the mistletoe and she'd let out a breathy moan, he'd nearly lost it. Stepping back before he did something crazy like slinging her over his shoulder and going belowdecks to find a free bunk, had been the sanest thing he'd done all evening.

Why was he even considering going along with such a ridiculous suggestion? Pretending to be a pirate at a formal New Year's Eve masquerade ball fell into the realm of a *Saturday Night Live* skit. "I've been thinking about your pirate suggestion."

Her smile disappeared and wariness returned to her eyes.

The solid ground beneath his feet began to shift and crumble. Noah knew, just as surely as he knew that the body contained 100-160 ml of cerebral spinal fluid, that if he backed out now, she would walk away.

He shoved aside his reservation and his good sense. "Yer suggestion, it be a fine one."

Noah wasn't sure which one of them was more surprised by the sentiment. He liked games well enough as long as they had well-defined parameters and clear, concise rules. Rules and standard procedures gave life order. Noah concluded his agreement to Josie's odd request illustrated that, contrary to what his family thought, he was very capable of being spontaneous. He could live on the edge. At least for one evening.

"I became a pirate because I love adventure," Josie confided in a hushed whisper, as if imparting a great secret.

They reached the edge of the dance floor and he took her into his arms. They began to move in time to the music.

"There's so much to see, to experience," she continued in an earnest voice.

Maybe it was having her in his arms or the fact that they were wearing masks. Perhaps it was being surrounded by music and the enticing scent of flowers that made it remarkably easy to play along.

They spent several dances discussing various places, er, *ports*, they'd visited. She seemed surprised he knew so much about Portland.

"Edward Jamison, a friend from my fellowship days, grew up there." Noah gave a nod of acknowledgment to a hospital trustee and his wife as he and Josie danced past them. "He's now practicing in Chicago."

"Great. Another doctor."

Though her tone was light, he noticed how the mere mention of the practice of medicine had her stiffening. There was only one thing he could think to do to dispel the sudden tension.

He whirled about in an intricate spin until she was breathless.

"There's a touch of pirate under that starched shirt." She grinned in approval.

While Noah knew that wasn't at all an accurate statement, he smiled and changed the subject.

"Your travels as a pirate have taken you far and near." He spoke softly, making sure no one dancing nearby overheard him saying the word *pirate*. "I'm curious how you found your way back to Jackson Hole."

Instead of tossing off some quick or clever response, she caught her lower lip between her teeth and appeared to carefully consider the question.

"Last year, a close friend—er, shipmate—was diagnosed with cancer. Not long after, I found a lump in my own breast."

Fear, hot and swift, struck him. He controlled his emotions and forced a casual tone. "Was it—"

"Benign."

With that one word, the knot that had formed in the pit of his stomach dissolved.

"My friend has a lot of stress in her life, some of it from unresolved family issues."

The sadness in her eyes had him pulling her a little closer. He resisted—barely—the urge to remind her that cancer had many causes. As a doctor's daughter and someone in the healing arts herself, that was something she doubtless knew already.

"Sasha's diagnosis and then my own breast lump, well, it was a wake-up call," Josie murmured, almost to herself.

He waited for almost a minute for her to continue before he prompted. "Because of your own family situation?"

"Yes."

Behind the mask, her eyes were hooded.

"Is the pirate queen home to stay?" He kept his tone deliberately light.

"Perhaps." The smile that lifted her lips didn't quite reach her eyes. "Tell me, Cap'n, how did ye end up in this landlocked port?"

"Moving here gave me the opportunity to work with your father and, more importantly, my family was here."

"You arrived what, about a year ago?"

He nodded.

"Do *you* plan to stay?"

It was a simple question. Undoubtedly she expected him to answer in the affirmative. Jackson Hole was a great place to live. Noah hesitated, thinking of the offer he had pending: the opportunity to go into partnership with his friend in Chicago.

Recently, he'd concluded if things remained at a standstill with Daffodil, it might be easier on both of them if he left town. But the decision to stay or go didn't have to be made now. He had until March to give Edward his answer.

Although his friend was in a well-regarded practice in Northwestern, the group had recently voted to tie themselves to one of the large health systems. Edward wasn't happy with the change. He wanted to go out on his own but needed a partner to share call. Noah was his first choice.

The deadline to accept or decline the offer was March 1. That was why Noah had decided to give reconciling with Daff one final, full-court press. If his efforts continued to be met with a brick wall, he could leave with the knowledge he'd done everything possible to bridge the gap between them.

"Noah?" Josie prompted. "It's not a difficult question. Are you planning to stay?"

"Who knows what the future holds?" It was the type of ambiguous answer he detested, but an honest one.

Noah was spared from saying more when the man Josie had kissed earlier—psychologist Liam Gallagher—tapped him on the shoulder and cut in. Though it was a reprieve of sorts, as he left the dance floor, Noah realized he'd prefer to be subjected to Josie's interrogation than turn her over to Liam.

"Looks like something is going on between you and my little sister."

Noah didn't bother to turn his head. The deep voice of Josie's brother, Benedict, was as familiar as a member of his own family. Since Noah had arrived in Jackson Hole last year they'd worked closely on many cases requiring the talents of both a skilled neurosurgeon and Ben's orthopedic surgery specialty.

When Noah had contemplated a move to the area, he'd been pleased to join a practice with surgeons of the caliber of Ben, Ben's father and Dr. Mitzi McGregor, their associate.

Tension filled the lengthening silence, leading Noah to deduce the comment hadn't been rhetorical. "Josie is a nice person."

Ben's gaze remained focused on his sister. "She's a bit of a flake. I can't see her being your type."

The dismissive tone coupled with the sentiment shouldn't have bothered Noah. Then why did he, a civilized man who'd never struck anyone in his life, feel like ramming his fist into Benedict's face?

"That comment shows how little you know your sister."

"You think *you* know her?" Ben gave a harsh-sounding laugh. "She disappeared right after her junior year in college. Sent this vague message that she had to find herself. It was almost a year before we heard from her again."

Noah opened his mouth but Ben continued without giving him a chance to speak.

"We didn't know whether she was dead or alive. My mother—" Ben took a deep breath and let it out slowly "—well, the worry nearly broke her."

The strain in his voice told Noah that Dori Campbell wasn't the only family member who'd worried.

He couldn't imagine what had possessed Josie to hurt her loved ones in such a way. He was certain her parents and brother only wanted the best for her. Just as he wanted the best for Daffodil.

If his sister had listened to reason, listened to *him*, she would have walked away from that loser Cruz Newton. She wouldn't be divorced and paying off his debts.

"I can sympathize with your frustration. My sister never listened to me." Noah clenched his jaw when Liam whispered something in Josie's ear, making her laugh.

"Their lives would be so much better if they did."

Noah nodded in agreement.

"You two look as if you're plotting to take over the world." Poppy Campbell slipped her arm through her husband's.

"Not a bad idea. The world would be running smoothly if I was in charge."

Ben's comment made his wife laugh.

Dressed in a loose black sheath, Poppy was an attractive woman with sleek dark bob and green eyes. Her black-and-gold half mask suited her elegant style.

From the time Noah had joined the practice, Ben's wife had been pleasant, if a bit distant. Ben had mentioned once that Poppy's first husband had been a neurosurgeon and Noah had the impression he was paying for the other guy's mistakes.

Poppy inclined her head. "Who's the guy in the joker mask dancing with Josie?"

"Liam Gallagher," Ben answered. "The poor sap can't take his eyes off her."

"She does look especially lovely this evening." Poppy's tone reflected affection for her sister-in-law. "Blue is a great color on her."

Benedict simply shrugged.

The band launched into another slow number and Liam gave no indication of releasing his partner. That added to Noah's mounting irritation, as well as the fact that the psychologist continued to hold the pirate queen a little too close for Noah's liking.

"Excuse me." Without waiting for a response, Noah

strode to where Josie and Liam danced. He tapped the man on the shoulder. "I'm cutting in."

The psychologist, who'd been smiling down at Josie, turned. His gaze shifted from Noah to Josie then back again. "Too bad. I'm not ready to give her up."

"You don't have a choice." Noah lifted Liam's hand from Josie's shoulder and pulled her into his arms.

"What do you think you're doing?" she asked in a throaty whisper as he whirled her far, far away from the astonished psychologist.

"Being a pirate." Noah flashed a sardonic smile. "We see what we want and we take it."

Chapter Three

As the minutes ticked down to midnight, Noah experienced a surge of regret. Spending time with Josie and playing their ridiculous pirate game had made the evening fly by.

The band finished the set and took a break, no doubt gearing up for the playing of "Auld Lang Syne" when the clock struck twelve.

"That is the strangest cake I can recall seeing." Noah cocked his head and scrutinized the multilayered monstrosity that would soon be cut and served with champagne.

Jet-black layers alternated with pristine white ones and caught the eye first. A crooked clock on the front made one take a second glance. The glittery mirror ball made it difficult to look away.

"It's so creative." Josie's tone was filled with awe. "I wonder who made it?"

"That would be me."

Noah and Josie turned in unison.

A slender woman with wavy hair the color of burnished copper and eyes that appeared violet in the light held a glass of champagne. Like most in attendance, she still wore a mask. Edged in gold, the deep purple color matched her cocktail dress. Although flattering, the cut of the dress reminded Noah of something from an earlier generation.

The woman extended her hand to Josie. "I'm Sylvie Thorne. My business, The Mad Batter, is all about creating unique cake designs."

They'd barely exchanged introductions when Josie's gaze returned to the cake.

"I adore it," Josie exclaimed. "It's so unique. Do you do catering for smaller events?"

"Absolutely." Sylvie took a sip of champagne. She appeared cool and collected but Noah saw the eager gleam in her eyes. "What do you need?"

"I have an event next week. I promised to bring the dessert. I need something that will serve thirty." Something in Josie's tone told Noah she wasn't excited about the event. "I'd love to take one of your cakes."

Noah held silent while Josie and Sylvie discussed details and made plans to connect on Monday.

Sylvie strode off after giving them both an impromptu hug.

A smile lifted Josie's lips. "Sylvie and I are going to be good friends."

"The two of you just met."

"Sometimes you just know." Josie gave a little laugh. "We have a lot in common. For example, we're both new in town."

"You grew up here," he reminded her.

"That was a long time ago. The friends I used to have are married now. Some with kids. They have their own lives, different interests." She lifted a shoulder in a light shrug. "You know how that is."

He did understand. Almost everyone he associated with since moving to Jackson Hole was married or dating someone. At most gatherings he felt like a fifth wheel. He realized that was why tonight had been so enjoyable. It'd been nice having a fellow pirate at his side.

The thought made him smile. "Have you thought any more about my proposition?"

"You're certainly persistent," she said mildly.

"It's a pirate thing." He lifted his glass in a mock toast. "Whether searching for sunken treasure or convincing a beautiful woman to join forces with me, determination is key."

"Well, Cap'n." She looped her arm through his in a companionable gesture. "The answer is still no."

Noah stiffened. "I don't understand why—"

"Ten." The crowd roared as the countdown to midnight began.

By the time shouts of "Happy New Year" rang out in the mountain home, he'd covered her mouth with his.

When her hands rose to rest on his shoulders, Noah realized he wasn't going to give up. Eventually she'd agree to help him. For now, he could think of no better way to end one year and begin a new one than kissing a beautiful masked woman.

After the kiss ended, Josie had taken a shaky breath and willed her fingers to remain steady as she removed her mask. When she'd told Noah she needed to meet Pauline at half past midnight, he'd insisted they had time to share a piece of cake and a glass of champagne.

She hadn't realized how erotic it could be to actually *share* a piece of cake with a man. When his lips closed over that bite of cake and those glittering blue eyes met hers, she'd imagined that mouth closing over her nip—

Josie shoved the memory aside and refocused on her conversation with Pauline. After arriving home they'd taken seats in the parlor, a warm, inviting room where flocked wall coverings and rugs of the same deep green hue were accentuated with burgundy furniture edged in walnut.

Outside, snow continued to fall. Inside, the room was cozy with a fire blazing in the hearth. Pretty floral bone china cups held Pauline's favorite blend of tea, African Autumn. The cranberry-and-oranges flavor of the herbal rooibos made for a soothing drink, especially with the addition of a dollop of honey. Josie felt the last of her tension ease as she took another sip.

The conversation on the drive to Pauline's home had been laden with amusing anecdotes about the people her employer had interacted with over the course of the evening. Not once had Noah's name come up.

When Pauline asked for a report on her evening, Josie chose her words carefully. "It was difficult to recognize people, because of their masks."

She went on to tell Pauline about Liam and Sylvie, about running into her brother and Poppy. But when Pauline gazed at Josie over the top of her teacup Josie knew the moratorium on Noah Anson had ended.

"You've mentioned everyone but my grandson." Pauline's gaze turned sharp and assessing in the golden light of the richly appointed parlor.

"I ran into Noah. He was helpful. He pointed out several women and men who I wouldn't have recognized because of the masks."

It was a simplistic explanation but Josie had no intention of explaining something she didn't understand herself...

why she'd shared two very hot kisses and most of the evening with a man who was not her type.

"Did he ask you to help him reconcile with Daffy?"

"What do you think?" Josie's droll tone had Pauline chuckling.

"My grandson is nothing if not persistent." Admiration ran through the older woman's words like a pretty ribbon.

"The man is a bulldog." Josie sipped her tea. "He hammered home the same points he'd made previously."

"What did you tell him?"

"No."

Pauline lifted a perfectly tweezed brow. "Just…no?"

"It's best to be simple and direct." Even as the words left her mouth, Josie had to swallow a smile.

Keeping it simple would have been maintaining a distance. And kissing, well, locking lips, would never be part of any keeping-a-distance equation.

"I respect your right to make that decision." Pauline lowered her cup and pinned Josie with the blue eyes her grandson had inherited. "And to change it, if you later decide otherwise."

Josie smiled, tempted to tell Pauline that a surgeon was not her cup of tea. Because this particular surgeon was her employer's grandson, she simply lifted the cup to her lips, took a drink and changed the subject.

The last place Noah wanted to be on a snowy night in January was at Benedict Campbell's home watching a football game that had already been played. Only the fact that he'd already turned down numerous invitations had pushed Noah to accept this one.

As he trudged up the front walk he mused on what had been a disappointing year so far, beginning with Josie turning down his proposition for the second time only minutes after the clock had struck twelve. He'd been surprised. Heck, he'd been stunned. When he'd kissed her at midnight and she'd kissed him back with enthusiasm, he'd been certain of success.

What more could he have done to secure her cooperation? Hadn't he played the pirate game? Danced with her to romantic ballads? Eaten cake and drunk champagne?

Her refusal shouldn't have shocked him. He'd learned how unpredictable the female species could be, beginning back in high school with Sia Norton.

Sia, a perky brunette with a quick mind and big breasts, had made him so crazy he couldn't even concentrate on his studies. She'd also confused the heck out of him with actions more emotional than logical.

It was the same with Josie. Instead of accepting an offer that made perfect sense and would be mutually advantageous, she'd thanked him for a fun evening and strolled off, mask dangling from her fingertips, lips still swollen from his kisses.

Noah shoved the thought of those few seconds of unrestrained passion aside along with his irritation over his unreturned phone call and text. He told himself if reuniting with his sister wasn't so important, he wouldn't be giving the baffling woman a second thought.

It was a lie, of course. Josie Campbell was like an itch that needed to be scratched.

Playing pirates. The thought brought a smile to his face as he rang the bell of the two-story home in Jackson Hole's affluent Spring Gulch subdivision.

Even before the door swung open, sounds of laughter and conversation spilled out onto the porch. Noah squared his shoulders. It had been a long, tiring day. The last thing he felt like doing was socializing. He told himself he'd stay for an hour, then make some excuse to leave.

Poppy greeted him at the door, relaxed and smiling in a pair of gray pants and a red sweater. Several glittery bracelets encircled one wrist. If Noah hadn't known she was pregnant, he'd never have guessed.

The smile she flashed was as warm and bright as the gems on her arm. Based on her previous coolness, her friendliness surprised him.

"Noah, I'm happy you could make it." She ushered him in and pulled the door shut, closing out the brisk north wind. "I was hoping for better weather. Then again, this is Wyoming in January."

She gave a little laugh and took his coat.

Noah forced a polite, interested expression. "Ben said you're hosting a book club this evening."

Actually, the book club was one of the reasons Noah had agreed to come tonight. When Ben mentioned his wife and the other women would be busy discussing their latest read, Noah had known he'd be socializing with just guys. This was one evening where he wouldn't feel like a fifth wheel. And then there was the gourmet feast Ben had promised.

"We're discussing *The 48 Laws of Power* this evening. But we're eating first." The twinkle in Poppy's eyes told him she was well aware of exactly how he'd been enticed to attend. "If there's time at the end of the evening, I'm hoping to bring out the portable mic and do a little torch singing. Do you sing?"

Noah froze. "Ben didn't mention anything about singing."

Poppy stroked the cashmere of his coat now folded over her arm. "Didn't he? I'll have to speak with him. It's always nice for guests to be prepared."

The only place Noah ever sang was in the shower, or in church, when he attended. "What's torch singing?"

"Romantic ballads."

Noah's shoulders tightened. "I don't know any."

"No worries. We have sheet music." She turned toward the hall then paused to gesture in the direction of the back of the house. "The men are to the right, women to the left. Dinner is in fifteen."

Though Noah was certainly no coward, if Poppy hadn't been holding his coat hostage, he might have thought about making a break for it. One thing he knew for certain. If there was any torch singing tonight, it wouldn't be him center stage.

Even if Poppy hadn't told him which direction to go, the high-pitched laughter and feminine voices—seeming to all talk at once—would have alerted him to stay to the right.

Noah had expected Ben's home to be as precise and put-together as the man himself. But instead of elegant pieces of expensive furniture there were overstuffed sofas and chairs exuding a warmth absent from Ben's office at the clinic.

His associate's office reminded Noah of a page out of *Architectural Digest*. The light gray walls held signed prints. The rosewood furniture was all about style rather than comfort.

Poppy's influence, he mused, as he rounded a corner and came to an abrupt stop. "Josie?"

For a second she appeared equally startled. She was dressed more casually than Poppy. Blue jeans hugged her long legs while a thin sweater in hot pink clung to her enticing curves.

She lifted a brow. "Are you stalking me, Dr. Anson?"

Affronted by the ridiculous accusation, he stiffened. "Most certainly not."

If her widening smile was any indication, his haughty tone amused her.

She rested a hand on his shirtsleeve and gazed up at him with those clear blue eyes. He felt the sizzle of her touch all the way through the broadcloth.

"In case you haven't figured it out, I was teasing." Humor underscored her matter-of-fact tone. "I didn't expect to see you here, that's all."

Noah gestured with his head toward the roar of male voices disputing a referee call. "Ben invited me over to watch the game."

"The college championship? A game that was already played?"

He smiled, sharing the sentiment imbued in her dry tone. "He assured me the food would be top-notch."

"He's right about that." Josie rocked back on her heels, no longer seeming in such a hurry.

For the first time he noticed what she wore on her feet. "Are those *pink* cowboy boots?"

She grinned, lifted a leg and held it out for his inspection. "Don't you love them? Sylvie and I went shopping yesterday. She helped me pick them out."

"Sylvie?"

"The Mad Batter."

For a second Noah wondered if she was speaking some strange foreign language. That thought was far superior to the fear that he'd stepped through some rabbit hole and had lost his ability to process information. "Pardon?"

"The woman who did the cake for Travis and MK's New Year's Eve party," she reminded him.

Noah finally recalled the quirky brunette with the violet eyes. "The cake was strange-looking, but I admit I never tasted better. Is she here tonight?"

Josie shook her head. "She's not, but she made another cake for tonight. It's super cute."

When Ben had said the food would be top-notch, Noah

had assumed a meal would be served. Now he wasn't so certain. "Is that what we're having…cake?"

"Well, I could have it for the main course and enjoy every bite, but—" she continued at his pained look "—there are others who insist on something more nutritious."

Noah raised his brows.

"Lexi Delacourt is in charge of the entrée. She's a gourmet cook. Veal piccata is on the menu tonight."

Noah was acquainted with the social worker and her husband. Although Nick Delacourt's specialty was family law, he'd helped Noah's grandmother with several contracts related to her business interests. Noah had been impressed by the man's savvy and attention to detail.

"Do you like veal?"

The question seemed to come from far away. He couldn't take his eyes off Josie. Pretty in pink and sexy as hell in those tight-fitting jeans.

Noah stepped closer, placing a hand on the wall on either side of her, crowding her. She smelled sweet, like lilies. The barest trace of pink gloss shimmered on her full lips.

She made no move to get away, simply stared up at him with those clear green eyes.

He wanted to taste her, to see if that mouth really was as sweet as he remembered. He lowered his head, relieved when she made no move to turn away.

"Josie," Poppy called out. "Was everything okay with Jack?"

"He was fine." Josie slipped out from under Noah's arms just as Poppy strode around the corner.

John William, known as Jack to friends and family, was Ben and Poppy's very active two-year-old.

Poppy's speculative gaze took in the scene. She smiled at Noah. "Did you get lost?"

"I ran into Josie," Noah explained with an easy smile. "She was telling me what's on the menu for this evening."

"It's always incredible when Lexi does the entrée." Poppy placed a hand on her stomach. "I only wish I could enjoy food the way I used to."

"You will again." Noah spoke in the reassuring tone he used with his patients, then excused himself and continued to the back of the house.

"You didn't tell me he was coming." Josie kept her tone low, even when she was certain Noah was out of earshot.

Dear God, she'd almost kissed him again. What was it about the man? Whenever he was near, her good sense seemed to go on hiatus.

If Poppy noticed the hint of accusation in Josie's tone, she gave no indication. She merely lifted one shoulder in an elegant shrug. "We've invited him over on many occasions. This is the first time he actually showed up."

"My lucky night."

"Is having him here an issue?" Poppy's expression took on a look of concern. "If it is, I can talk with Ben and—"

"No." Because Josie had spoken more sharply than she'd intended, she softened the word with a smile. "It's just, for some crazy reason, when Noah is around the part of my brain that's capable of rational thought goes haywire."

They quickly reached the edge of the kitchen, where the other women were congregated. When Josie started to step inside, Poppy took her arm. "Do you like him? I heard you kissed him at the party Saturday night."

Josie hesitated. She settled for waving a dismissive hand in the air, and forcing a casual tone. "We shared a kiss at midnight on New Year's Eve. Noah is a nice enough guy, but not my type."

Poppy cocked her head. "Exactly what kind of man is your type?"

For a second her mind went completely blank. She could hardly diss Noah without also dissing her brother Ben. Josie thought of the men who'd been at the party the other night. No one stood out. Surely there had to be someone she could use to defuse Poppy's scrutinizing gaze.

"Liam Gallagher," she blurted out.

While the child psychologist hadn't made her heart beat the slightest bit faster when they'd danced, he appeared to possess many of the characteristics she admired.

"Liam." Poppy's perfectly painted red lips curved upward. "Good to know."

The gleam in her sister-in-law's eyes had Josie wondering exactly what she was planning.

Whatever it was, it didn't matter. The only thing that mattered was she'd gotten Poppy off the ridiculous notion that there was something between her and Dr. Noah Anson.

Chapter Four

It didn't take any time at all for Josie to realize she should have kept her mouth shut. About everything.

The evening's downhill slide began when the men piled into the kitchen to fill their plates with food from the sumptuous buffet.

Josie had been chatting with Mary Karen, a perky blonde who barely looked old enough to drink much less be the mother of five, when Noah strode into the room.

For a second she wondered if he planned to stay true to form and seek her out, but as he walked past with her brother, she realized they were deep in discussion about some new surgical technique.

Their total focus on the topic reminded Josie of the types of discussion that had occurred most nights around her parents' dining room table. Her three older brothers, all aspiring doctors, and her father would discuss medicine as if it was the most fascinating subject in the world.

Her mother, God love her, would feign interest. There was a time—back when Josie had been desperate for her father's love and approval—when she'd also listened attentively.

Occasionally, she'd forget her audience and bring up something she'd learned in yoga class. Although her dad hadn't rolled his eyes, usually one of her brothers would make a joke. They'd all laugh. Eventually she'd quit sharing.

A heaviness filled her chest at the memories, an unwelcome sensation she hadn't felt in a long time. Was she crazy for coming back and trying to rebuild a relationship? Perhaps it would have been better if she'd stayed in Portland and returned home only for the occasional Thanksgiving or Christmas holiday.

Though she'd come home to Jackson Hole filled with determination and enthusiasm, she had to admit she still had no clue what made her father and brothers tick. If she couldn't understand them, how was she ever going to form a connection?

While adding a spoonful of each salad to her plate, Josie listened to Mary Karen chatter about her oldest set of twins, then found a seat at the large oval table.

Cassidy Duggan, owner of the Clippety Do-Dah Salon—and Daffodil's boss—stopped on her way back to her seat to ask Josie who'd designed the cake she'd brought that evening. Cassidy was absolutely convinced her twin daughters would adore a unique cake for their upcoming birthday.

After giving the hair salon owner Sylvie's contact information, Josie lifted the glass of iced tea to her lips, feeling as out of place as she'd been at the New Year's Eve party. Did everyone in this book club have kids?

She let her gaze search the room, mentally cataloging

those in attendance, and realized, yes. Tonight, everyone in attendance were parents. Except…

From across the room, her gaze met Noah's. He smiled.

Blood flowed through her veins like warm honey.

Josie told herself she didn't want Noah to sit in the empty chair beside her. Of course, it *was* a free country and if he happened to choose that seat, she could hardly ignore him. In her mind she began to plan all the topics they'd discuss, none of which involved teething, dance classes or children's birthday parties.

Noah was still filling his plate when Poppy placed a hand on the chair next to Josie's and announced, "There's a spot for you over here."

Josie shifted her gaze to find Liam Gallagher headed in her direction. She amended her earlier assessment. Apparently there were three of them without children here, not two. When she slanted a glance at her sister-in-law, Poppy offered a benign smile.

"You can thank me later." Her sister-in-law leaned over and whispered in her ear.

Liam pulled out a chair and smiled warmly. "May I sit next to you?"

"Absolutely."

Josie discovered Liam was an interesting conversationalist, full of humorous stories about all the places he'd lived before returning to set up practice as a child psychologist in Jackson Hole.

She attempted to keep Liam talking, even while casting surreptitious glances in Noah's direction, but the psychologist refused to monopolize the conversation. To her chagrin, he kept redirecting everything back to her. He listened intently to whatever she said, so intently she felt as if she was in a therapy session and should request a bill at the end of the evening.

When Cassidy passed by them on her way to get a piece of cake, Josie seized the opportunity to redirect the psychologist once again.

"I heard Tim and Cassidy started dating after a bachelor auction," Josie commented, praying Liam would take the ball and run with it.

"It's true." Liam rested an arm against the back of her chair in a casual gesture that had Poppy smiling in approval as she refilled their glasses of iced tea. "Actually, Tim was filling in for me that evening. I had a bad allergic reaction and couldn't participate. Cassidy was the high bidder. They fell in love, got married and had a baby boy. The rest is history."

"It's strange how life works," Josie murmured, thinking of her own journey back to Jackson Hole.

This time her gaze settled on her brother. She watched as he slipped his arm around Poppy's waist and took a heavy glass pitcher from her hands. Whatever he whispered in her ear made her smile.

Benedict seemed different—softer—when he was around his wife. Still, his brusque words when she'd returned told her he hadn't changed, not really, not enough. Not nearly enough.

"People don't change." The words came out on a sigh.

"They can."

Josie inhaled sharply and jerked her attention back to her right. Instead of Liam, Noah sat beside her, a piece of cake and a cup of coffee in front of him.

"You're not Liam."

"Very perceptive." He forked off another bit of cake. "This is excellent. Try a bite."

Before Josie was even aware what was happening, the fork that only moments before had been in his mouth, was in hers. Shades of New Year's Eve. The taste of butter and almonds and sugar melded in a sweet explosion.

"It's very good." She handed the fork back to him. "Now tell me what happened to Liam. Did you bury him in the basement?"

"I believe he grew tired of being ignored and went in search of greener pastures."

"I wasn't—" Josie paused, flushed.

She hadn't ignored the psychologist, she thought defensively. Still, she had let her mind wander. It was a bad habit. One she thought she'd successfully broken.

"I need to apologize." She began to rise but Noah's hand on her arm had her sitting back down.

"I was kidding." Noah took another bite of cake. "Liam received a call from his answering service. A patient was in crisis and he had to leave."

"He didn't say a word." Josie wasn't sure if she felt indignation or relief.

"He probably didn't want to disturb your reverie."

She swatted his arm, but Noah only grinned. The boyish smile had her going warm all over. For the first time since she'd walked through the door, she let herself fully relax.

After all, she had no desire to try to impress Dr. Anson with her wit and charm. Absently, she took a bit of her own piece of cake. It wasn't simply good, it was stellar.

A bell sounded, a gentle tinkling.

Beside her, Noah cocked his head. "What is that?"

"Five-minute warning for the men to leave the kitchen."

Noah forked off another bite of cake, seeming in no hurry to leave with the other men. "The hospital is holding a post-Christmas event for their medical staff Saturday night."

"My dad mentioned something about it." Josie gazed at

him speculatively. "I told him it appears the medical staff isn't very important to the hospital."

He frowned, much the way her father had done. "What makes you think that?"

"Think about it. They made no effort to fit the party in during the actual holiday season."

"They were being accommodating. Everyone is busy over the holidays. Attendance will be higher in January when there aren't as many demands."

The last thing Josie wanted was to engage in a conversation about anything medical. Still, recalling the experience with Liam, Josie kept her focus on Noah. Though, she had to admit, her attention rarely wandered when she was with Noah. But she knew if she got too close, she'd get burned.

Yet the intoxicating scent of his cologne, the square cut of his jaw and those intense blue eyes called to her at a primal level. Even more disturbing was the realization that it only took one flash of his smile to have something low in her abdomen tightening.

This physical attraction was what made him so dangerous. It would be too easy to get wrapped up in physical desire and forget one basic fact; this man was cut from the same bolt of cloth as her brothers and father.

"—go with me."

Josie turned toward Noah just as Poppy announced the men needed to leave the kitchen so the book club could begin their discussion.

"Anson," Ben called out. "Unless you're going to join the ladies, it's time to clear out."

"Give me a call this week." Noah squeezed her arm and rose. "We'll work out the details."

After placing his coffee cup and plate in the sink, he joined the exodus of men, leaving Josie to ponder how he'd managed to slip away without her having a chance to tell him no.

Well, she'd darn well decline his offer later tonight. Before he stepped one foot outside of this house, she'd make it clear there was no way she was attending any function with him, especially one of the medical variety.

"It's Thursday." Sylvie sat across the table from Josie at the Hill of Beans coffee shop. "The event is Saturday."

Josie grinned at the baker. "Thank you for orienting me to the date."

As she predicted, she and Sylvie were well on their way to becoming friends. Her gut told Josie she could trust Sylvie to be discreet. It was good to have someone with whom she could share her feelings. As much as Josie liked and respected Pauline, the woman was Noah's grandmother.

"I'm going to call him today." Josie picked up her phone from the table, glanced at the time, then set it down. "The yoga class I'm teaching at the church starts in an hour. I'll call him after that."

Sylvie took a sip of her latte. "Why not now? Get it out of the way."

"Ben mentioned he and Noah have a big surgery today. If I call now I'll just get his voice mail."

The baker's gaze remained focused on Josie's face. "I'd say that would make this a perfect time."

"Calling when I know he's busy is a coward's way." Josie lifted her chin. "Contrary to what my brother thinks, I'm not a coward."

A group of teenage girls tumbled into the shop, laughing and talking loudly, distracting her from the troubling thought.

"You don't seem like a cowardly person to me." Two

lines appeared between Sylvie's brows. "Why would your brother say such a thing?"

"They stopped by my parents' house last night—Ben, Poppy and Jack." Josie had felt a surge of envy at the sight of the happy family. "They brought over the ultrasound of the baby."

"That's cool." Sylvie hesitated. "Isn't it?"

"Everyone is so excited. Even my dad. Poppy and he have this great relationship. It's almost like she should have been his daughter." Recalling the big hug her father had given Poppy, Josie had to swallow past a sudden lump in her throat.

"I still don't get the coward comment," Sylvie persisted.

"Have you ever run away from something?" Josie asked her. "Because deep down you knew if you stayed you'd end up being talked into doing something you'd regret?"

"Yes." Sylvie's face went stark white. "I have."

"Well, that's why I left college after my junior year and took off." Josie began to shred the napkin between her fingers. "I knew if I stayed I'd end up going to medical school like everyone else in my family. Only instead of loving it like they had, I'd hate it. I *had* to leave."

"When you leave unexpectedly—" Sylvie's gaze shifted out the window where snow fell in large picturesque flakes "—no matter how good the reason, most people will consider you a coward. What those people don't realize is that making a decision to leave takes a lot of strength. It's often easier—safer—to take the path of least resistance."

Josie considered what Sylvie said and felt some of the weight lift from her chest. Here, finally, was someone who understood. "I would have hated myself if I'd have stayed."

"As would I." The sadness in Sylvie's eyes told Josie she didn't have the market on suffering.

"What happened?" Josie rested a hand on Sylvie's arm. "If you don't mind my asking."

"Much the same as what happened to you. I was a square peg trying to fit into a round hole. When I realized it wasn't going to work, it was best for everyone I left."

"You left your…family?"

"My fiancé."

Something in the baker's eyes told Josie not to push for more. "I'm sorry."

"It was the hardest thing I've ever had to do." Sylvie lifted her chin, her violet eyes shimmering with determination. "But, like you, I was smart enough to know it was best to leave."

Josie nodded. She only wished the thought gave her comfort. "Last evening, Ben tossed out that he hopes if they have a girl, she never treats Poppy the way I treated my mom."

Sympathy filled Sylvie's eyes. "Ouch."

"My dad told Ben to drop it." Josie pressed her lips together. "He didn't, of course, arrogant jackass. Asked me why I didn't just stand up for myself. He told me only a coward would run off and break her mother's heart."

Josie wasn't sure what she expected Sylvie to say. Perhaps agree with her that her brother was a jerk. Or maybe soothe her by repeating she'd made the best decision possible. Instead, her new friend remained silent for a long moment.

"It's hard for me to understand people who have such a different personality than I do." She smiled at Josie. "I bet in Portland you surrounded yourself with men and women who pretty much viewed life through a common lens."

Josie frowned.

"I do it, too," Sylvie said before she could respond. "That's why you and I became friends."

The tension gripping Josie's shoulders eased.

"It's like my dad and brothers speak a different language," Josie admitted with a rueful smile. "We look at the same situation and arrive at far different conclusions."

A shadow passed over Sylvie's face. "It's very frustrating."

"I want to understand them." Josie lifted her hands, let them fall. "And I want them to hear—and understand—me. Sometimes I think I need an interpreter."

Instead of laughing at the ridiculous thought, Sylvie's expression grew thoughtful. "Yes. I believe that might be helpful."

Josie gave a little laugh. "Too bad I can't simply snap my fingers and conjure one up."

"You don't need to do that, not when you have the perfect person at your disposal." Sylvie leaned back in her chair smiled. "Noah Anson wants something from you. You need something from him. From where I'm sitting, it's a match made in heaven."

Chapter Five

Saturday night, standing at the door to his grandmother's house, Noah faced his sister. While he knew Daffodil frequently visited Pauline, it was rare for him to run into her here.

"Good evening, Daffodil." He studied the younger sister who'd gone from worshiping him to not being able to stand the sight of him.

The pretty little girl had grown into a striking young woman. With her petite frame, blond hair straight and loose to midback, and big blue eyes, she could have been the poster girl for a 1960s flower child. The fact that she had a propensity for wearing all organic clothing only furthered that image.

Daffodil had been one of the top students at the boarding school where she'd been dumped after their parents' divorce. After graduation, instead of going to college as he'd hoped, she'd become a hairstylist.

That had been the first in a series of mistakes she'd made, all because she'd refused to accept his guidance.

"Who's at the door?" Pauline's voice carried from the back of the house.

The fact that he was chilled while wearing a wool top-coat told him his sister must be freezing in her bare feet and loose-fitting cotton pants and collar-less shirt.

"It's Noah," Daffy called over her shoulder then stepped aside. "Come in."

Her tone was deliberately careless, rather than rude. Still, Noah absorbed the punch.

He didn't like feeling helpless and ineffectual. That was exactly how he felt around Daffy. Dealing with her was incredibly frustrating. No matter how calmly and logically he responded, she bristled.

At this rate, they'd never reconcile. Though Noah knew plenty of men with little or no contact with their siblings, Pauline and Daffodil were basically his only family. Though he maintained a cordial relationship with his parents, they both had new spouses. He and Daffy had long ago been relegated to their past.

Daffodil gestured with one hand. "Gram and Josie are in the parlor."

"Perhaps you and I could grab dinner one night?" Noah suggested.

Daffy turned toward the stairs. "I don't think that'd be a good idea."

"Look, Daff." Noah placed a restraining hand on her arm. "Forget that I was right about Cruz. That knowledge gives me no pleasure. As far as I'm concerned, that's in the past."

His sister jerked her arm back. Anger flashed in her eyes, but for a moment, a second, Noah caught a glimpse of another emotion. One that looked like regret.

Then she was gone, a blur of blue and yellow disappearing up the staircase.

Noah waited until his sister disappeared from sight before strolling into the back parlor. His grandmother had a cheery fire blazing in the hearth. She sipped a cup of tea while Josie sat on a nearby settee.

Josie wore a dress of cherry red for tonight's medical staff festivities. Sexy, razor-thin heels of the same color completed the look.

She'd pulled her blond hair back in a twist that showed off a slender elegant neck and ears that shimmered with tiny ruby teardrops.

"Noah." Pauline rose and opened her arms to him.

When he stepped close, his grandmother rested her hands on his forearms and studied him.

Though in her midseventies, Pauline could pass for a woman ten years younger. An active, vital widow, she was relaxed and comfortable in her own skin. A pleased look filled her blue-gray eyes.

"Some men are made to wear black tie," she pronounced, then turned to Josie. "Don't you agree, my dear?"

His date for the evening rose in a single fluid movement. "I agree. Your grandson looks quite dashing this evening."

"As much as I'd love for you both to stay and visit, I don't want you to be late for the party." Pauline's smile widened to include Josie. "The way you look tonight, Noah is going to have to fight to get one dance with you."

Josie's face colored with embarrassment. "Oh, Pauline."

"Gram is right," Noah said, finding the thought irritating, which made his words clipped. "That dress is very…"

Provocative was the word that came first to his mind, but he substituted "lovely," which didn't do the dress, or her, justice.

Pauline walked them to the door and brushed a kiss across Josie's cheek. "I won't wait up."

The gesture of affection, directed toward someone his grandmother hadn't known all that long, surprised and puzzled Noah.

He opened the door to his Range Rover and helped her inside, inhaling the sweet, tantalizing scent of her perfume.

Strictly business, he reminded himself.

Noah wheeled the car from the curb. "I was surprised to see Daffodil."

"Pauline invited her to spend the night." Josie slanted a glance in his direction. "Daffodil is fighting a cold and your grandmother is convinced she isn't getting enough sleep. I think she wanted to give her granddaughter some TLC."

"Gram likes to baby Daffodil." Noah turned onto the highway in the direction of the Spring Gulch Country Club. "I don't understand why Daffy doesn't live with Gram. It's expensive to rent or buy in Jackson Hole and Gram has plenty of room."

"I didn't move in with my parents when I moved back," she pointed out.

Noah inclined his head. "Why didn't you?"

"I thought it'd be too hard for us to relate as adult to adult if I was living under their roof. It'd be too easy for us to fall back into a parent-child role."

"Yet, you live with my grandmother."

"She offered me a room at a fantastic rate. Plus, she's not my parent."

Noah pondered Josie's assessment. His sister was obviously determined to be seen as an adult. Since she was now, what, twenty-six, it made sense. Which meant he needed to adjust how he responded to her. He only wished he knew how to do that…

"You love your sister." Though Josie spoke the words as a statement, he heard the question.

He pulled the vehicle to a stop under the elaborate stone overhang frontage of the Country Club, answering her before he stepped out. "Of course."

She slipped from the passenger side after a valet in gray pants and long topcoat opened her door.

Rounding the front of the vehicle, Noah handed the keys to the smartly-dressed man, then took Josie's arm. Though the area under the overhang was dry, those heels of hers were wicked and it didn't take much imagination to visualize her taking a tumble and sustaining a head injury.

Once inside they checked their coats, then strolled down the large foyer to the ballroom past huge planters overflowing with fresh flowers. A sweet scent filled the air. Up ahead the sound of big band music accompanied by the clink of fine crystal and laughter could be heard.

"I'm not good at these things," Noah confessed. As a teenager, he'd enjoyed the challenges of math and science rather than sports and parties. As a young adult, his career path had taken up his time and energy.

Oh, he'd become socially adept but he'd never found anyone he trusted enough to share his deepest emotions. For him, trust came hard. The way he saw it, opening himself up to someone was tantamount to giving them a hand grenade along with instructions on how to pull the pin.

His high school girlfriend had taught him this lesson when she shared with her friends *everything* he'd told her.

"I prefer smaller events."

Noah pulled his thoughts and attention back to the beautiful woman at his side.

Josie stopped at the edge of the ballroom and glanced around the room filled with men in black tie and women in cocktail attire. "There will be a lot of people we both know here tonight so it should be…fun."

He wondered who she was trying to convince. Noah lifted a brow.

She swatted his shoulder. "Yes. Fun."

"If you say so."

"Think about it. Who I don't remember, you'll know. And I can give you the scoop on anyone who's grown up here."

Her prediction held pinpoint accuracy. Noah had attended a number of these events since his arrival in Jackson Hole last year. Each time, he'd smiled at the appropriate moments, made casual conversation with colleagues and then headed home. Enjoying himself, specifically having *fun*, hadn't been on tonight's agenda.

While he'd had previous conversations with Mayor Tripp Randall, and his wife, Adrianna, there was much he hadn't known about the couple. Over dinner he learned "Anna" was a good friend of Ben's wife, Poppy, and that Tripp had been a hospital administrator on the East Coast before returning home to Wyoming.

"Jackson Hole is really a big small town," Josie commented as the four of them chatted amiably. "Everybody knows all the news practically before it happens."

Anna Randall offered a rueful smile. "That's so true. I'd heard all about you and Noah spending time together at the New Year's Eve party so I wasn't surprised to see you together."

"My darling wife hears everything." Tripp gazed at her with fondness. "I count on her to keep me up-to-date."

Anna colored. "I'm not a gossip."

"Of course not, sweetheart." Tripp quickly backpedaled, his expression contrite. "I simply meant—"

"—that as a midwife, you keep your finger on the pulse of the community." Josie offered Anna a warm smile.

"Exactly right. You've got yourself a sharp one, Anson." Tripp gestured with his head toward Josie. "Better watch yourself."

Noah gave Josie an assessing glance and smiled. He needed her help reconciling with his sister. The fact he found her easy to be around was an extra bonus. Yet, Tripp was right. He needed to watch himself around her.

Anytime he'd ever lost his head over a woman, his well-ordered world had been thrown into chaos. He'd vowed not to put himself in that position again.

It was a promise he meant to keep.

Josie could be impulsive. She readily admitted the weakness. Deciding that Noah Anson was exactly who she needed if she was going to reconcile with her parents and brother might, on the surface, appear impetuous. But she was convinced—or almost convinced—it was the right decision.

When Noah pulled her into his arms for some pre-dinner dancing, she decided this was her opportunity to hammer out the details of the "deal" she was prepared to propose.

The problem was, when his arms slid around her and he pulled her close, strategizing became the last thing on her mind. She fit against him perfectly, the top of her head just under his chin.

His chest was broad, his arms strong. For a surgeon, physical endurance was almost as important as knowledge and talent. Standing for long hours, maintaining control of motor skills was essential. But now, with Noah's arms around her, Josie was only conscious of how good he smelled and how safe she felt in his arms.

For a woman who'd prided herself on handling every aspect of her personal life, the realization she could so easily relinquish control—even on the dance floor—was vaguely disturbing.

Not disturbing enough, however, to pull out of his arms. She let herself relax, determined to enjoy the evening. When her friend Sasha had become ill, Josie had been reminded that each day was a gift to be treasured.

The call to dinner in the adjacent ballroom sounded and Josie moved with Noah to the other room. It would have been easy to become separated but Noah kept a hand on her arm.

After gazing over the sea of round linen-clad tables, she turned to Noah. "Is there assigned seating?"

"Not tonight." Tripp came up behind them. "If you don't already have a table chosen, there's still room at mine. Right over there, where Anna is already seated."

Noah accepted and Josie found herself soon seated between Noah and a woman whose husband was on the hospital's board of trustees. With just a sprinkle of gray in her light brown hair, Marjorie Martin looked like someone her mother might know.

When she asked, she discovered her mom and Marjorie played mah-jongg every Wednesday afternoon.

"And what is it you do, my dear?" The woman deftly cut a piece of sirloin.

"I do a little bit of everything," Josie told her. "Right now I teach yoga at First Christian three times a week. I also work as Pauline Bettinger's assistant. In addition I'm also a licensed massage therapist looking for space to set up my table."

"I understand completely."

"Pardon me?" Josie asked politely, sensing Noah had

finished his conversation with Tripp and shifted his attention back to her.

The woman smiled. "I dabbled in a lot of things, too, while waiting for Mr. Right. I don't understand why so many women are determined to build a career. I can't imagine a finer job than being a wife and mother, can you?"

Josie wasn't sure if she should be amused, or insulted. Though she barely knew Marjorie, it was apparent the woman had a kind heart. Instead of taking offense, Josie patted her hand. "Being a good wife and mother is indeed a worthy undertaking."

She and Marjorie chatted for several more minutes. Then Tripp got up and made a speech, followed by remarks by one of the trustees. Dessert was served, then everyone was dismissed for dancing.

Noah tugged her into his arms and they began to dance. "Just waiting around for Mr. Right, eh?"

Josie stiffened at the teasing tone. "If I was looking for Mr. Right, believe me, this wouldn't be the venue I'd choose to do my searching."

"Why not?" Noah sounded genuinely puzzled. "I would think this would be prime hunting grounds."

When she only blinked, he added, "There's quite a few single doctors in attendance this evening."

"I'd never marry a doctor." The second the words left her mouth, Josie wished she could pull them back.

If she'd just taken a moment to think before speaking, there were a dozen other ways she could have answered. "Not that there, ah, is anything wrong with your profession. I mean, some women would love to marry a physician. I'm just not one of them."

Amusement sparkled in his blue eyes. "Understood."

She half expected him to ask why she felt that way, especially since her family tree was heavy with doctors. He didn't say a word.

They danced in comfortable silence, the sweet music spilling over Josie, washing away her tension, leaving her languid and relaxed.

"I've been thinking some more about your proposition." Josie let her eyes close for just a second as the music embraced her.

"I'm happy to hear that." His palm slid up her spine, making her shiver.

"I—I actually believe we can be of mutual benefit to each other."

His palm stilled its downward journey. "Really?"

She waited to speak again until the stroking had resumed. Then, sighing with pleasure, she laid it all out for him.

"Let me get this straight." After the song ended, he took her hand and guided her to a small alcove off the main ballroom where the music and noise were dulled. "You'll help me with my sister, if I help you with your brother and dad."

Josie nodded, impressed he'd been able to condense everything she'd said during the last song into two sentences. "That's the gist."

"I'm in practice with your father and brother." His brows pulled together. "That makes what you're proposing… awkward."

She blew out a frustrated breath. "You'd simply be giving me pointers, helping me interpret their actions and suggest alternate responses to their comments."

"Still—" He rubbed his chin.

"How is it any different than what you're expecting me to do with Daffodil?"

"I wanted you to convince her she should listen to me."

Josie narrowed her gaze. "You *said* you wanted me to convince her you're a good guy."

"That's what I said."

"It isn't the same at all," she said pointedly. "That's why you need me."

"I don't need you. I don't need anyone." His words came out in a hot rush.

She arched a brow.

His jaw set. "What I need is your expertise."

"Ditto." Then because she didn't want him to think she was hot for him, Josie clarified. "Let's get one thing clear. I'm not personally interested in you, Anson. You're not my type."

"You're not my type either."

To Josie's surprise, his mildly spoken words stung.

"For the sake of this proposition, we'll need to at least be cordial while we consult with each other," Josie told him.

"Date."

"What?"

"We'll need to be cordial while we date."

"Who said anything about dating?" Josie took a step back, out of the range of the spicy cologne that had been tripping her heart all evening. "There's no reason for us to…date."

Her tongue felt thick, the word awkward against it.

"I disagree. If we date we'll be able to observe firsthand the reactions of our family members and thus be able to offer more valuable and constructive feedback."

While Josie had made the suggestion they utilize each other's expertise, she'd never once thought of the time they'd be together as *dating*. "We can meet weekly, tell each other exactly what was said."

His mulish expression had more words tumbling out.

"We can meet more than once a week," she amended, "if needed."

He continued to shake his head. "As much as that plan would make it easier on both of us, there's built-in error."

"How?"

"Your interpretation of what was said will come through when you relay a conversation. That could influence the advice that I might give. If I observe the interaction first-hand, I'll be detecting both verbal and nonverbal clues."

Josie straightened her spine. "I would never doctor what I said to make myself look better. If you're suggesting that I would, I—"

"We tend to see things through the filter of our own experiences and viewpoints," His gaze met hers. "That's why you and I are having such difficulty achieving our goals. Why we find it necessary to enlist each other's help."

"I suppose that makes sense," Josie grumbled even as she forced a smile and offered a friendly wave as Mitzi McGregor and her husband, Keenan, strolled past.

"Not simply any independent observer would do," Noah continued. "You and Daffodil have similar personalities. I share many characteristics with your brother and father. That gives us the ability to offer each other a different perspective."

"How long do you think this whole thing will take?"

"No idea." Noah lifted his hands, let them fall. "I hope not long."

Josie nodded. "We probably should start soon."

"Your parents just walked in." Noah held out a hand. "We'll start now."

After a moment of hesitation, Josie placed her palm against his. She hoped this was one deal she wouldn't regret.

Chapter Six

As she crossed the ballroom with Noah, Josie wondered why her father hadn't mentioned he was attending the event this evening and why he and her mother had showed up so late.

Once she and Noah reached her parents, it didn't take long to find out.

"He hit a tree head-on. Just turned seventeen yesterday." John Campbell shook his head then went on to describe the boy's injuries.

Despite her dad's use of medical terms, Josie understood most of what he said. For those first three years in college she'd taken all the science courses required for medical school admission. Each summer she'd returned home to help out in her father's practice.

Though some of her experiences during the summer breaks had been interesting, and the Anatomy and Physiology courses proved beneficial for yoga and massage, the practice of medicine had never been her calling.

"We saw Poppy and Benedict leaving." Her mother's brows drew together in worry. "Poppy said she was feeling extra tired this evening."

Josie shook her head. "Running after a two-year-old while pregnant has to be exhausting."

As if he'd just noticed her standing there, her father turned and focused those steely blue eyes on her. "Since you're not working, perhaps you could stop by and help her out."

Josie bristled. "I am wor—"

Noah's hand tightened around hers. He slanted her a pointed look.

She took a second to settle her emotions, then smiled and spoke in a pleasant, but firm, voice. "I'm working two jobs now, but my hours are somewhat flexible. I'll give Poppy a call first of the week, see what I can do to help out."

To Josie's surprise, her father reached over and squeezed her shoulder. "I know she'll appreciate the offer."

She and Noah visited with her parents for several more minutes before they were able to gracefully exit and make their way to the dance floor.

Noah pulled her into his arms.

"Why did you tell me to shut up?"

He chuckled. "Trust me. That's something even I wouldn't dare."

"You nearly crushed my fingers."

"Guilty on that charge." His smile flashed and she felt her irritation ebb.

"Why did you do it?"

He glanced around.

She did the same and noticed several speculative glances aimed in their direction. Even if they kept their voices low, there was a chance they could be overheard. "We'll talk about it later."

It wasn't exactly a hardship to spend the rest of the evening dancing, sipping champagne and making small talk with Noah and anyone who crossed their path.

For her part, Josie kept the conversation light. She noticed Noah did the same.

Though she didn't know the neurosurgeon any better by the time the valet pulled his vehicle to the door, tonight had shown her they could tolerate each other's company.

"We should debrief," Josie advised as Noah turned the SUV toward the highway. "Revisit the evening, analyze and interpret, discuss ways to improve."

"It's best to do it right away while the memories are still fresh."

She nodded. "Let's start with why you squeezed my hand."

"We'll talk about that once we get to my house."

"Your house?"

"The only private place at my grandmother's would be your bedroom."

Josie cringed, imagining telling Pauline she was taking Noah up to her room so they could *talk*. No. That definitely wouldn't do.

Josie straightened in her seat. "We can talk now. In the car."

He shook his head. "Analysis can't be short-changed. We need to totally focus. That's difficult to do while driving, especially with ice on the roads."

The headlights illuminated the sheen on the road ahead. With a reluctant sigh, Josie settled back against the warm leather seat.

Minutes later, he turned onto a residential street in the Spring Gulch subdivision.

"You live here?"

"You sound surprised."

"I am. I mean I'm not." She lifted a hand, waved it distractedly. "It doesn't matter."

He slanted a sideways glance. "For this partnership to work, we need to be honest with each other."

"Okay. I am a bit surprised." She took in the sprawling homes on large lots. "This is a family area."

"I don't like condos or townhomes." He wheeled the Land Rover into the driveway of a rambling ranch faced with stone. The garage door slowly lifted. "I wanted space and a place that felt like a home. Besides, property in this area is a good investment and I can use the tax break."

"Now, *that* I believe," she said and made him laugh.

The door to the three-car garage closed silently with the press of a button. Once inside the house, Noah took her coat then motioned for her to take a seat in the great room.

Josie chose an overstuffed chair by the fireplace. Because she wasn't looking to impress her host, she immediately slipped off her shoes and reached down to rub the arch of her foot. Then, because she was slightly chilled, she grabbed a black cashmere throw from the back of the chair and wrapped it around her.

"I'd say make yourself at home." She turned to see Noah smiling at her from across the room, "But it appears you already have."

"My feet hurt."

"I could rub them for you?"

She thought he was joking, but couldn't be certain. "Thanks, anyway."

He only smiled and she wondered if he was doing that mind-reading thing again. "May I get you something to drink?"

"I've already had enough champagne." She tilted her head and thought for a moment. "I could be tempted by something hot."

"How about hot chocolate?"

"Perfect." Josie flung off the blanket and stood, leaving her shoes behind. "I can help."

She followed him into the kitchen. When he pulled a tin of cocoa from the cupboard, she raised both brows.

"The milk is in the refrigerator." Noah placed a saucepan on one of the gas burners.

When she didn't move, he frowned. "Problem?"

"I thought you meant you'd pull a packet from a box and heat some water in the microwave."

"This won't take long," he said, obviously misunderstanding her comment.

"You can make hot chocolate from scratch?"

"It's not brain surgery," he said with a wry smile.

Josie chuckled.

"Daff loves it…or she used to, anyway." His eyes took on a faraway look. "It would always upset her when our parents fought, so I'd make it for her. Her job was to dump in the marshmallows."

"That was a nice big brother thing to do." Josie recalled how lonely she'd felt when Benedict, the brother closest to her in age, had been sent off to an out-of-state prep school. "Ben was good to me when I was a kid. He was the one who taught me to snowshoe."

The pleasant memory brought with it a warmth toward Ben she hadn't felt in years.

Josie took a carton of milk from the side-by-side refrigerator and watched Noah add sugar, cocoa and a dash of salt to some hot water.

"Your father was exhausted tonight," Noah said amiably as he continued to stir the mixture. "Once this comes to a boil, I'll need a quart of that milk."

Searching the cupboards, Josie quickly discovered a measuring cup and calculated she'd need four cups. She stood in readiness at Noah's side, the pleasant scent of cocoa filling the air. "We might as well start the debriefing now."

He nodded. "That would be most efficient."

"I don't understand why you stopped me from reminding my father that I do have a job, two jobs in fact."

"As I said, John was exhausted. He'd just finished a multilevel fusion, which likely means he was in the OR for seven hours. Then he had to come home, grab something quick to eat and head to the party."

"Perhaps he should have simply skipped the event."

"From what I've observed, your mother enjoys these types of functions."

"You're saying he didn't want to disappoint her."

"That would be my guess." Noah slanted a glance at Josie. "It's boiling. We'll give it a couple of minutes and then add the milk."

Josie hefted the milk carton into one hand and raised the measuring cup with the other. "I'm ready."

His approving smile made her feel all warm inside.

"Back to our wrap-up." Josie fought to stay business-like. "You believe it was best not to confront my father with inaccuracies simply because he was tired?"

"I believe your father is aware of your position with my grandmother as well as the yoga classes you teach at the church. Clearly, he doesn't count either of those positions as a real job. And he was exhausted. No matter what you'd have said tonight, it wouldn't have mattered."

Like the mixture in the saucepan, Josie's blood began

to bubble. "I can't believe you think that just because my father had a rough day, I shouldn't stand up for myself."

By the time the last word left her mouth she was sputtering and furious.

"Time to add the milk," he said mildly.

When she simply continued to stare as if he'd spoken in a foreign tongue, he took the carton of milk from her hands. He measured then added the liquid to the pan.

Only after he'd begun to stir did his gaze return to her. "He's worried about Poppy."

"He likes her." The churlish tone of her voice made Josie wince.

"She's his daughter-in-law and the mother of his only grandson."

"He admires Poppy, respects her." Josie turned away from Noah's searching gaze. "Forget about her. We're talking about what happened tonight."

"It's all relevant." With one fluid gesture, Noah removed the pan from the heat, shut off the flame and tossed in some vanilla extract without bothering to measure.

When he handed her a whisk she stared blankly at the cooking utensil.

"Whisk the mixture until it's foamy," he ordered, in the same autocratic tone she'd often heard come out of her father's mouth. "I'll get the marshmallows and the mugs."

Josie's fingers tightened around the utensil, tempted to hand the wire whip back to him and insist he take her home. Instead, she began to whisk the mix into a froth, taking her irritation out on the innocent mixture.

Noah returned seconds later with two large brown mugs and a bag of marshmallows.

Deciding she might as well have a sip or two before heading home, Josie took the cup he offered her. Instead of returning to the living room, she took a seat at the small wooden table overlooking what she assumed was the backyard.

At the moment it was dark and snowing so hard it was difficult to see past the falling blanket of white.

"I don't think this is going to work."

He took a seat opposite her and raised a brow.

Josie couldn't resist taking another sip of the chocolate. The rich taste slid down, heating her all the way to her toes. "We see things too differently."

Noah drank the cocoa, his long fingers wrapped around the mug. He leaned back against the back of the chair and studied her. "I thought that was the point."

When he looked at her with those brilliant blue eyes, Josie found it difficult to think. "But—"

"Before you make any decision, I suggest you finish listening to my assessment and consider my recommendations."

Josie scowled, but couldn't think of a good reason *not* to listen. She took another sip of the delicious cocoa. "Go ahead. Wow me with your analysis."

The sparkle in Noah's eyes told her he was amused by her calm dismissal. That only irritated her more.

"I've noticed you and John have similar personalities."

Josie made a sound of dismissal. "My father and I are nothing alike."

"Studies have shown that most successful orthopedic surgeons are motivated more by a desire for personal development rather than money." He lifted a brow. "Sound familiar?"

Josie shrugged.

"They believe in keeping physically fit. You're into fitness." He smiled. "You teach yoga."

"Minor similarities."

"You're both stubborn."

Josie couldn't deny the charge but his comment could be taken as a criticism of her father. "Are you saying my dad is stubborn?"

"At times." Noah surprised her by taking her hand loosely in his. "Trust me. Tonight wasn't the night to argue with him. He was tired—physically and emotionally. He's also worried about Poppy. My advice would be to pick your battle times."

"I didn't plan to argue with him." Josie placed her cup on the table, tugged her hand away. "I was simply going to explain that I *do* work."

"Which he already knows." Noah pushed back his chair and stood, then began to pace. "Think about it, Josie. If you were exhausted, would that be the best time for your father to come to you to discuss issues of any importance?"

She wanted to say yes, if for no better reason than she wanted him to be wrong. Yet, even in the interest of preserving her dignity, she couldn't lie.

"You were right to stop me." She expelled a weary sigh. "If I'd pushed, it would have ended in an argument. Nothing would have been resolved."

"We need to have dinner with your parents. Soon." Noah's eyes met hers. "After you've called Poppy and asked what you can do for her."

"I'd have helped her, anyway." She lifted her chin, daring him to disagree. "I don't need anyone pushing me."

"Great. That part should be easy."

"What's the deal with dinner?"

"It doesn't have to be a meal. I simply need time to observe more interactions between you and your father." Noah stopped pacing and sat down.

"I don't like my dad acting as if I'm some kind of slug." Josie thought she'd done a good job of speaking calmly but even a deaf person would have heard the hurt.

Noah shifted his gaze out the window, seemingly focused on the falling snow. "Perception is everything."

"I don't understand."

"I believe the words are self-explanatory."

"Not to me. Then again, I'm not a doctor." The second the childish taunt left her lips, Josie wished she could pull it back.

Noah turned to her and his impassive gaze flickered over her face. "If you want to be taken seriously by your father and brother, you need to rebuild their perception of you. How would you like them to view you?"

Josie sighed. "I'd like them to see me for what I am—a strong, hardworking and determined woman who can be counted on to do the right thing."

"Good. How do you believe they view you?"

A knot formed in the pit of her stomach. "As a flake who takes off running when things get tough."

To her horror, her eyes filled with tears. She quickly blinked them back, lifted the cup of chocolate to her lips. She took a long sip and the action steadied her. "How does your sister view you?"

A muscle in his jaw jumped. It took only a second for Noah to respond. "I have no doubt Daffodil would call me an overbearing jerk who thinks he has all the answers."

Josie blinked. Oddly, the harsh assessment made her feel more connected to Noah. She sipped her cocoa, forced a casual tone. "How would you like her to see you?"

He lifted his chin. A shadow of stubble darkened his cheeks and she realized the man had really nice-looking lips, firm, smooth and well-sculpted. She wondered if they'd taste like chocolate tonight. Or perhaps…marshmallows.

Determinedly she pulled her gaze from his mouth, just as he spoke.

"I'd like Daffodil to see me as a concerned brother who cares about her welfare."

It was a tall order. But no less high-reaching than her own goal. *Dream high or go home.*

Her lips curved in a slight smile. "You know what, Noah?"

"What?"

"I think we have our work cut out for us."

Chapter Seven

If Noah had known the condition of the roads when they'd left his house, he'd have insisted Josie spend the night. It had been snowing even before they left the Country Club. That wasn't surprising. It was January in Jackson Hole. Heavy snowfalls were practically guaranteed.

When he'd made the decision to settle in Wyoming, Noah had traded in his car for a Land Rover with four-wheel drive. Despite the AWD, the roads in this area were often treacherous.

Josie had remained quiet on the drive to his grandmother's house, letting him concentrate on the road. When he finally pulled into the driveway, she let out a long sigh of relief.

He'd barely pulled the key from the ignition when she turned in her seat to face him, one hand on the door handle.

She hesitated for a second. "I'd like you to text me when you get home. That way I'll know you made it home safe and you're not in a ditch somewhere."

Noah nodded, surprised how good it felt to have someone concerned about him. "I'll walk you to the door."

The wind whipped the snow into mini cyclones. Noah kept a firm grip on Josie's arm. Though it was apparent she had a great sense of balance, her wickedly sexy heels on the scooped path already covered with ice crystals was an accident waiting to happen.

He waited while she pulled out the key from her small bejeweled evening bag. Before she could insert it in the lock, the door swung open.

Pauline motioned them inside.

"I can't stay, Gram. I was simply making sure that Josie made it—"

"Get inside," Pauline snapped, looking regal despite the fluffy blue robe and slippers. "You're letting in all the cold air."

Noah told himself there was no reason he couldn't exchange a few cordial words with his grandmother before getting back on the road.

Pauline shut and locked the door behind him.

Noah raised a brow. "Afraid someone is going to break in while we're standing here talking?"

"You're staying the night." Pauline, who'd already taken Josie's coat, held out her hand for his.

Why was it that he found his eyes settling on Josie, who now stood behind Pauline, her lips curved in a slight smile? That only confused him more.

"There's no need. I—"

"They just closed the highway," Pauline declared. "Only essential personnel are supposed to be out."

He'd driven quite proficiently in far worse conditions since moving here. Not like his sister, who always wanted to brake when a car began to skid.

Daffodil.

His gaze shot to his grandmother's face. "Did Daffy make it home safely?"

"She never left. She's upstairs, hopefully asleep." Worry filled Pauline's eyes. "She still has a cough, poor lamb. I made her some tea with honey and put her to bed in one of the guest rooms."

"Shall I check on her?" Josie spoke for the first time since they'd stepped into the warmth. "I could make sure she doesn't need anything while you attempt to convince Noah to stay."

"Thank you, dear." Pauline patted her shoulder. "But I was just up there. She's sleeping."

Noah considered his options. Daffodil was here. It had been a long time since he'd spent any time under the same roof with her sister. With Josie and Gram here to run interference, this might be the chance he'd been waiting for…

"You've convinced me."

Relief spread across his grandmother's face. "You're the smartest grandson I have."

"I'm your only grandson," he said with a wry smile. "Unless you have an objection, I'll put the Land Rover in your garage."

In answer, his grandmother pulled a remote from a small drawer in a side table and handed it to him. "I'll have a nice hot cup of tea waiting for you."

After taking a few seconds to release the locks, Noah stepped into a blizzard. As he brushed the snow from his eyes and strained to see two feet in front of him, Noah realized staying the night really had been a wise decision.

"Did they really close the highway?" Josie tried to keep her voice casual as Pauline hung her coat in the hall closet.

Pauline looped her arm through Josie's as they strolled back toward the kitchen.

"The roads are treacherous. According to the forecaster,

the snow is supposed to fall all night." There wasn't a hint of apology in Pauline's gaze. "My grandson is safer staying here."

"It's convenient, too."

Pauline arched a brow.

"Tonight you have both your grandchildren under one roof."

"I imagine one of the reasons Noah was so agreeable was because this will give him a chance to interact with Daffodil." Pauline shook her head. "Even after nearly two years the girl is still angry with him. I don't believe they've had a civil conversation since he tried to stop her wedding."

"You're thinking the reason he decided to stay is to have access to her?"

"Either that or access to you," Pauline said in a matter-of-fact tone.

Josie gave a little laugh. "To me?"

"I may be past seventy but I'm not blind. Noah is enchanted by you."

Perhaps Pauline thought she'd be thrilled to hear the prominent doctor was interested in her. The truth was, if Noah was interested in her, she'd have to break their agreement.

She believed Pauline was mistaken. This was purely a business arrangement between her and Noah. Yes, she'd admit—but only to herself—to a certain…sizzle…between them. But that was only on a purely physical level.

Though the only thing Josie wanted at the moment was to go to bed, she knew Pauline would be offended if she cut the evening short. Once Noah returned, Josie carried the cup of tea into the parlor. She took a seat in the carved walnut parlor chair, leaving Noah and his grandmother to share the settee.

The way he looked at her, with that little smile on his

lips, told her he was aware her seating choice wasn't a random act.

Josie lifted the cup and focused on Pauline. "What do you think is wrong with Daffy?"

"It's the tail end of that crud that's been going around." Pauline sighed. "Cough and fatigue primarily, although I suspect from her flushed cheeks she was running a slight fever this evening."

Noah inclined his head. "Did you take her temperature?"

Pauline waved a dismissive hand. "Her cheeks were slightly pink, not red, so even if she did have a fever it couldn't have been that high."

"Common sense medicine." Josie grinned. "I love it."

"You would," Noah said dourly.

She cocked her head.

Pauline leaned forward and patted her hand. "I believe my grandson is simply saying that you and I are women blessed with an abundance of common sense. Isn't that right, Noah?"

The man was no fool. When you find yourself on stormy seas and someone tosses a life preserver in your direction, you take it.

"Exactly right, Gram."

If he saw Josie roll her eyes, he gave no indication.

The older woman took a sip of tea. "How was the party?"

"Nice," Josie said politely.

"Same as all the others." Noah glanced at Josie. "The band was good."

Josie nodded.

Silence descended for a moment, broken only by the crackling fire and the clink of china cups against saucers.

"How was book club the other night?" Pauline asked, apparently determined to make conversation.

"We discussed *The 48 Laws of Power*." Josie tried to think of something positive to say about the book. "I guess it was a good primer for learning how some people think. It was a bit too dark for me."

"Life can be dark." Noah sipped the tea his grandmother had handed him. *"The only means to gain one's ends with people are force and cunning."*

"Johann von Goethe. The quote is from the book." Josie wasn't sure why she was surprised. "You read it."

"I did." He took another sip of tea.

"I didn't like the message." Josie pulled her brows together. "Crush your enemy completely and all that."

"Some people live by that philosophy," Noah mused. *"The 48 Laws of Power* can also be used to spot people who are dangerous and only out for themselves."

The conversation reminded her of those halcyon days on the high school debate team. Josie's heart began to trip. She placed her cup on a table near her chair and leaned forward, fully engaged.

Unlike what her father believed, she'd never been averse to friendly discourse. She'd simply wanted him not to do all the talking. She longed for *her* thoughts to be heard, she wanted a chance to express beliefs supported by logic.

While Noah clearly held a differing opinion about the book, she enjoyed listening to his perspective. At book club, the other women merely agreed it was too dark, then had moved on to another round of desserts and wine.

The evening had been lovely, but Josie hadn't done much thinking.

After about ten minutes, Pauline rose and announced she was retiring for the evening. She and Noah paused in their discussion only long enough to bid her good evening, then returned to the book.

Finally, they noticed their tea was cold, the fire barely

simmered in the grate and they were still dressed in their evening finery.

Josie stared at him thoughtfully for a long moment. "I believe you're right."

"On which point?" He grinned. "I've made so many good ones."

She rolled her eyes.

"Getting a different perspective on any issue is valuable." Not sure if she was speaking about the book or the insights he could offer about her father, she added, "You have something to offer me."

"I believe I do."

"I have something to offer you, too." Josie took a deep breath and let it out slowly, hoping she wasn't going to regret this choice. "If the proposition is still on the table, I'm in. I'll help you with your relationship with Daffodil, if you help me with my brother and father."

He smiled, or was that a smirk? "I knew you'd eventually agree with me."

"Excuse me. Each of us helping the other was *my* idea."

He waved a hand, as if that was of no consequence.

Josie shut her eyes and counted to three. Working with this arrogant doctor was going to be a pain in the rear end.

She just needed to figure out why she was looking so forward to it.

Noah planned to sleep in, then hopefully spend time with his sister over a leisurely breakfast of eggs, toast and juice.

The knock on the door of the guest room his grandmother had designated as his sounded at 7:00 a.m. Ignoring the noise, Noah rolled over.

There was another sharp rap on the door, more loudly

this time. "Noah. Church is in forty minutes. You need to get up. I don't like to walk in late."

He groaned aloud. One of the few mornings he got to sleep in and his grandmother wanted him to go to church? Hadn't he gone with her at Christmas?

While a refusal was poised on his lips like a high diver ready to take the plunge, Pauline added extra incentive to the request. "Daffodil, Josie and I are having breakfast before we leave. If you hurry, you might have time to eat, too."

Noah threw back the duvet. There was no way he wasn't going now. This was the perfect opportunity to work on getting through to Daffy. She couldn't walk away from him if they were in church. Not only that, this would give Josie a chance to observe any interactions between him and Daffodil.

It'd be easier if breakfast and church was only about his relationship with his sister. But Noah admitted he was also looking forward to seeing Josie this morning.

After a three-minute shower, he felt almost human. Though he stored some clothes here, the selection was severely limited. He pulled on a pair of gray pants, a charcoal-colored dress shirt and a pair of dark loafers and hurried downstairs.

Daffodil and Josie sat at the kitchen table, giant mugs of coffee and plates of half-eaten pancakes before them. Pauline stood behind the stove wielding a spatula, a fluffy white apron protecting her red dress. She brightened when she saw him.

"I have two blueberry pancakes with your name on them."

Noah poured himself a cup of coffee from the percolator his grandmother had owned since Elvis Presley ruled the airwaves. He took a long drink of the strong brew and felt nearly human. "Do we have time?"

"If you eat quickly." Pauline flipped a golden-brown cake with well-practiced ease. "Sit beside your sister."

Noah pretended not to see Daffodil flinch as he pulled out the chair and sat. He offered an easy smile. "How are you ladies this morning?"

"Fabulous. I slept great." Josie's gaze shifted pointedly to Daffodil.

When his sister continued to not speak, Noah prodded. "Are you feeling better this morning, Daff?"

The silence stretched until Noah wondered if she had decided not to speak with him this morning. It was just the sort of childish behavior he'd come to expect from her.

His temper rose.

If she thought acting like a child would get her anywhere in life she was sadly mistaken. He opened his mouth to remind her of what happened the last time she behaved like a child and wouldn't listen to reason.

The feel of Josie's bare foot against the side of his leg had Noah inhaling sharply. A punch of lust erased the words from his lips.

His gaze shot to her. Her lips were rosy, her eyes bright. Was that desire reflected in those piercing green depths?

The stroking abruptly stopped and Josie gave an almost imperceptible shake of her head.

It took him a moment to realize she wasn't coming on to him. She wanted him to keep his mouth shut.

Noah fought a surge of disappointment. Taking a breath, he forked off a bite of the pancakes his grandmother had placed before him.

"I am feeling better." Daffodil finally spoke, her gaze meeting his.

While there was little warmth in her expression, she'd

spoken directly to him in a polite manner. He couldn't recall the last time that had occurred.

Progress.

"Glad to hear it." He took another bite of pancakes then offered a benign smile. "There's been a lot of viruses going around. It's taken some of our office staff nearly two weeks to get over it."

Pauline patted her granddaughter's shoulder. "Well, I'm going to continue to pamper my girl until she's back to 100 percent."

"Thank you, Gram." Daffodil's soft whisper held a wealth of emotion.

A knife stabbed his heart. His sister was so grateful for any comfort offered. He cursed his parents—and himself—for failing to make such a sweet creature feel loved.

But regardless of what Daffodil believed, he loved her. Very much.

Noah took a gulp of coffee in an attempt to wash down the lump in his throat. He'd just regained control of his emotions when a blast of air rattled the windows.

"I'm not certain attending church is wise." Noah frowned. "The roads might still be closed."

Josie gave a dismissive snort. "How long have you lived here, Anson?"

"The wind is still gusting at times but the snow stopped just after 4:00 a.m.," his grandmother explained. "The plow went through about an hour ago."

Noah remembered his first winter in Jackson Hole, recalled the pile of snow and ice left at the edge of his driveway after the plow went down the street. "Do I need to shovel us out?"

Pauline untied her apron and hung it on a porcelain hook. "Already done. Jerry Davis, my handyman, came over with his snowblower and cleared the drive."

Josie smiled around her fork. "Kind of the opposite of 'you snooze, you lose.'"

"I would have happily done it," Noah insisted.

"Happily?" Josie laughed. "Yeah, right. Relief is written all over your face, *doctor*."

Daffodil stilled beside him.

Instead of the sharp response that his sister likely expected, Noah chuckled. For some reason, he continued to find Josie's impudence appealing.

"Time to go," Pauline announced in a decisive voice before he could zing Josie back. "I refuse to be seated in the back row."

Noah warmed up the Range Rover for the drive to church. Pauline sat in front with him, while Josie and Daffodil took the backseat.

Hearing his sister chatting animatedly with Josie and Pauline filled Noah with a feeling of well-being. Maybe, just maybe, with Josie's help, they could be a family again.

Noah met Josie's gaze in the rearview mirror...and smiled at the promise reflected in the clear green depths.

Chapter Eight

Josie caught the stares of the parishioners as she walked into First Christian with Noah. Too late she realized she should have thought through Pauline's invitation a little more carefully. Especially when she caught sight of her parents. Seated next to them in the full pew was Ben and his family.

As they passed by, her father's eyes widened momentarily. Almost immediately a pleased look crossed his face. In addition to a warm smile, John Campbell offered a nod of approval.

Josie felt her spine stiffen, one vertebra at a time. It was true she desperately longed to mend her relationship with the men in her family. Still, she didn't want that approval to come only because they thought she was dating one of their kind.

She jerked her arm from Noah's light hold but the effort came too late. She'd been seen, judged and found worthy, all because she was "with" a doctor.

The usher, a man with a full beard and warm brown eyes, had been several years ahead of her in high school. He showed them to a pew near the front of the sanctuary. Noah stepped back to let her enter first. Josie thought Daffodil would follow her but Pauline waved Noah forward.

There was barely enough room for the four of them. The usher watched until they'd jammed themselves into the allotted space.

Noah's muscular thigh pressed firmly against the pencil skirt Josie had pulled on that morning. She'd coupled her latest purchase with a fuzzy azure sweater that made her eyes look more blue than green.

Glancing unseeing at the church bulletin in her hand, Josie idly wondered if her dad would have been as pleased if she'd walked into church wearing the same dress she'd worn to the party last night. Her lips lifted into a rueful smile.

Knowing her father, if he thought she'd "caught" herself a doctor, he'd probably break out that special bottle of wine he'd purchased last year for an astronomical sum.

Her arrangement with the neurosurgeon suddenly left a sour taste in her mouth. As the minister welcomed them from the pulpit, Josie considered when to tell Noah she'd changed her mind.

Noah's fingers closed around her arm in a firm grasp. In one smooth movement she found herself hauled to her feet. Furious at being manhandled, Josie jerked away, nearly clipping the jaw of her retired third-grade teacher in the process.

"Sorry, Mrs. Sandburg." Josie offered the startled woman an apologetic smile then turned back to Noah. Despite her irritation, she kept her voice low. "What do you think you're doing?"

Before he could answer, Josie realized everyone around them—including Mrs. Sandburg—had risen.

Looking amused, Noah slid the hymnal in front of her.

Josie sighed and, with a toss of her head, began to sing. She expected their voices to clash like an out-of-tune violin. To her surprise they blended as smoothly as cream over whiskey, creating a pleasant harmony.

As they moved to the second verse, the tightness in Josie's shoulders eased. She'd discovered long ago there were some places where it was simply impossible to hold on to anger: a yoga studio, a massage table, a church pew.

But the calm didn't last. Not when Josie had only to turn her head to see the pew where her family sat, radiating approval. This uncomfortable alliance with Noah needed to end. Once the service concluded, Josie would tend to that matter.

The minister's booming voice filled the church. Josie tried to listen but had difficulty concentrating. Not only was Noah's leg pressed intimately against hers, he smelled absolutely terrific.

The intoxicating scent wasn't expensive cologne but shampoo and plain old soap and water. He'd obviously showered but hadn't taken the time to shave.

With an appealing stubble darkening his cheeks, Noah reminded her more of a sexy bad boy than a prominent physician. It would have been easier if he was simply a sexy bad boy. If he was, she wouldn't have to end their relationship, er, business arrangement.

Of course, if he was a bad boy, he probably would be of little use to her in helping her with her family. It was definitely a no-win situation. For the third time that morning, she heaved a heavy sigh.

When Noah reached over and took her hand, she attempted to pull away but he held tight. His sardonic smile made her realize he'd morphed into a sexy pirate bad boy when she wasn't looking.

The man was definitely trouble. When his thumb began to stroke the soft center of her palm and her heart tripped, Josie accepted he was not only sexy, but dangerous.

He released her hand when they rose for another hymn. As the song ended, she crossed her arms, keeping her hands firmly out of reach.

While the minister's sermon held everyone else spellbound, Josie continued to have difficulty concentrating. Her thoughts tumbled like an out-of-control tilt-a-whirl in her head. She'd been so convinced coming home was the right decision. Now she wasn't so sure.

Perhaps she should simply have maintained a cordial relationship with her family from a distance. Many people her age rarely spoke to their parents or were estranged from one or more siblings.

"Sometimes you have to know when to fold," she murmured to herself.

"It's too early to give up," Noah said in a barely perceptible whisper.

"You don't know what I'm thinking," she whispered back, earning the fish-eye from her former teacher.

"Sorry," Josie mouthed to the woman then, like an obedient schoolgirl, shifted her gaze to the front of the church.

She tuned out everything but the sermon. When the minister's words registered, Josie nearly groaned aloud. What were the odds? The minister spoke on new beginnings.

Noah elbowed her. "How appropriate."

Josie ignored him. She kept her gaze on the pastor.

He chuckled, then leaned close, his breath warm against her ear. "Ignoring me won't work."

Despite Josie's best efforts, his teasing tone made her lips twitch.

As if seeing her smile as encouragement, Noah rested his arm on the pew, above her shoulders.

She pretended not to notice.

When Pastor Johnson mentioned it was in struggle true change occurs, Josie found herself nodding and realized she wanted the reconciliation with her family to be successful.

She couldn't quit trying. Not yet.

For the rest of the service, she made a concerted attempt to pay attention. All too soon, they rose and waited to be ushered out. She heard Noah ask Daffodil what her plans were today.

"I'm working at the salon." Daffodil covered her mouth with a tissue and coughed. "I need to make up for calling in sick yesterday."

"You're still sick."

Daffodil visibly tensed at the censure in his voice. "I feel good enough to put in a few hours."

"I have an appointment this week," Josie interjected into the tense silence, lifting a strand of blond hair. "Maybe I'll have you cut all this off when I come in."

"I hope that's a joke." Noah sounded shocked.

Josie batted her lashes at him. "I guess you'll just have to wait and see."

Daffodil inclined her head, studied Josie. "If you're in the mood for a change, we could alter the color, too."

Noah blanched. His gaze shifted between his sister and Josie. Suspicion clouded his gaze. "Seriously, is this a joke?"

Daffodil shot him a dismissive glance. "Like Josie said, I guess you'll have to wait and see."

* * *

Noah dropped off Daffodil at the Clippety Do-Dah salon, then Pauline at her home. Josie had accepted a last-minute invitation from her brother to join him and his wife for breakfast at the Coffee Pot.

Though she'd eaten a short stack of pancakes in his grandmother's kitchen less than ninety minutes earlier, Josie immediately accepted the offer.

Accepting the invitation made sense. From her look of pleased surprise it had obviously been a long time since her brother had asked her to do anything. When Noah had begged off, something he saw in Ben's face made Noah wonder if the offer had been more for him than Josie.

Noah hoped he was mistaken. In the parking lot, Josie split off from him to go with her brother and sister-in-law. But when Noah glanced back, he found her gaze on him.

She'll be fine, he told himself. The knowledge that he wanted to remain with her told him turning down Ben's offer had been the right move. There would be other times, other opportunities, to assess the interaction between Josie and Ben.

Yet, instead of turning his vehicle in the direction of Spring Gulch and home, Noah soon found himself back in downtown Jackson.

This wouldn't be his first time meeting friends and colleagues who gathered at the popular café while their kids were in Sunday school. For as long as Noah had been in Wyoming, the large table at the back of the café had been reserved for this group of young professionals, the movers and the shakers of Jackson Hole. Occasionally there was another single man or woman, but most were couples.

While Noah had a standing invitation, he wasn't into the couples scene. After securing a parking space not far from the Coffee Pot, he strode down the recently scooped sidewalk with a spring in his step.

Today, he wouldn't be alone. Neither would Josie.

Noah's smile disappeared when he caught sight of Liam Gallagher.

The child psychologist was holding open the café door for an elderly man and his blue-haired wife. Noah had no doubt he and Liam had the same destination in mind.

"Gallagher." Noah called out the greeting as Liam ignored him to follow the couple into the café. "Not going to hold the door open for me?"

"If I wasn't a gentleman, I'd let it slam in your face." Liam offered an affable smile at odds with the sentiment. "I'm not feeling particularly charitable after that stunt you pulled last night."

Noah feigned innocence. "What stunt?"

"You stole my dance partner."

"She was mine first." Noah gave a careless shrug. "Besides, she prefers me to you."

"In your dreams." Liam laughed. "I have it on good authority *I'm* the type of guy Josie is looking for."

The psychologist's bold confidence told Noah there might be some validity to the words. Everything inside Noah stilled. "What good authority?"

His tone came out casual and a bit disinterested, just as he'd intended.

"Poppy said Josie let it slip that she was interested in me."

Noah ground his teeth together, but was precluded from answering when the table came in sight.

Already three-quarters full, there were several empty seats, including one next to Josie. With the determination that had been a part of him since he'd learned to walk at a young age, Noah rounded the table with one destination in mind.

Noah didn't care what Josie had supposedly told Poppy. He and Josie had an arrangement. While they did, they were a couple. Noah was not about to let anyone, especially Liam Gallagher, intrude.

He caught Josie's expression of startled surprise when he brushed a kiss on her cheek then claimed the chair next to her.

Casting him a dark look, Liam was forced to take a seat farther down the table beside Mitzi McGregor, one of Noah's partners.

Ben—seated on Josie's other side—stared unblinkingly at Noah. No doubt he had questions. About the kiss. About the fact that less than fifteen minutes earlier Noah said he wasn't able to be here.

"Change of plans," he said with a flick of his hand in answer to Ben's unspoken question.

As expected, his colleague said nothing. But Noah knew tomorrow, when they saw each other at the clinic, Josie's big brother would have questions. That was okay. By then, he and Josie would have their stories straight.

Explaining they were now a couple would take care of most of the questions. The kiss, well, their relationship had to appear realistic so that others—he slanted a pointed glance at Poppy—didn't disturb the rhythm by attempting to match-make.

The older woman making her way around the table, notepad in hand, was the same waitress who'd waited on them each time Noah had joined the group. He remembered the orange lipstick, wiry gray hair and the efficient, nononsense manner. Aware that most of the couples needed to be through in time to pick up their children, the woman made quick work of taking their orders.

Without even glancing at the menu, Josie requested a yogurt parfait and coffee.

"Poached egg and toast," Noah said when the waitress glanced at him. "No coffee."

While his grandmother's pancakes were second to none, Noah preferred to start his day with protein.

The waitress wrote down the order. She gazed speculatively at Noah, jerked her head toward Josie. "Are you two together?"

A sudden silence descended on the table. Out of the corner of his eye, Noah caught Liam's interested expression.

"We are," he said with a decisive nod. "Put her order on my check."

Josie opened her mouth to protest. Then, seeming to recall their arrangement, she shut it without speaking.

Conversation resumed and the waitress moved on.

"I didn't realize the two of you were dating." Ben's sharp and assessing gaze fell on Noah. "I couldn't believe it when I saw you walk into church this morning together."

"I was surprised, too." Poppy leaned forward and focused on Josie. "You never said—"

"It's early days," Josie hurriedly responded before Noah had the chance. "Noah and I are still in the getting-to-know-each-other phase."

"I take that to mean you're not...exclusive?" Poppy slanted a glance in Liam's direction.

Determined to shut down that train before it left the station, Noah closed his hand over the one Josie had resting on the table and squeezed. It was surprisingly easy to add an affectionate look. "Actually, we've decided to go the exclusive route. It's easier to get acquainted when there aren't a lot of...distractions."

He glanced at Josie seeking confirmation. This was it, he thought. In or out. Noah was well aware that he wasn't the kind of guy she preferred, but he could prove useful. Just as she would be useful to him in his quest to mend his relationship with his sister.

How she responded would tell him just how important reconciliation with her family was to her. If she backed out now, he'd continue on his own. Unfortunately, he didn't have much time left. If Daffodil remained resistant to his overtures, he decided he'd accept the position in Chicago at the end of February.

He refused to stay in Jackson Hole, hoping for a reconciliation that might never happen.

"I think our decision makes a lot of sense," he heard Josie say. "Noah and I are both busy people. Our free time is limited. This way we'll spend it together."

The suspicious look in Ben's gaze hadn't dimmed. If anything it had become more pronounced.

"What's really going on here?" he demanded, his gaze firmly fixed on his sister.

She gave Ben a cool look. "I don't know what you mean."

Those piercing gray eyes that held the power to make interns quake, settled on his sister. "What kind of game are you two playing?"

It was so close to the truth that Noah felt a surge of admiration for Ben's acuity. A second later he felt Josie's arm slide through his. She glanced up at him with laughing eyes.

"Noah and I share certain…passions. We both enjoy games." Her voice turned sultry. If Noah didn't know they'd only kissed, he'd be convinced the games she referred to were X-rated. "All sorts of games. Want to hear—"

"Enough." Her brother's hand sliced the air. "I don't want to hear about any perverted stuff you're doing with Anson."

"You asked." She gazed up at her brother all wide-eyed.

"Forget it." Ben took a slug of coffee.

But Noah couldn't forget it, *wouldn't* forget it. Though Josie's comment appeared to have allayed her brother's suspicions, it cast her in a bad light. Her remarks made it look as if he was interested in her only because of sex.

It didn't matter she'd been the one to give the impression. Josie was worth more, much more, than that and he would make that very clear.

"She's jerking your chain, Ben." Noah kept his voice flat, his gaze steady. "I'm with your sister because I enjoy her company. She has a quick mind and a wicked sense of humor."

"You made all that up?" Ben's gaze shot to Josie. "For what purpose?"

She wrapped her fingers around the ceramic mug. "It was what you expect from me. You don't believe I'm smart or clever enough for any accomplished man to take me seriously."

"I never said that," Ben huffed, looking indignant. But something in his eyes told Noah that Josie had hit the mark.

Sadness flitted across her face but was gone so quickly Noah wondered if he'd only imagined it.

She lifted her chin. "When Noah indicated we were dating, your only comment was to ask what kind of game we're playing."

Ben had the decency to look abashed. "Accept my apologies."

"It's just that it's so unexpected," Poppy interjected in a futile attempt to pull her husband out of the fire. "Hearing that you two are an item."

"Really?" Josie's eyes remained cool. "Noah and I were together at the Fishers' New Year's Eve party. We spent time together at your book club. We attended a party at the country club last night. This morning it was church."

"You said he wasn't your type." Poppy spoke in a hushed whisper, casting an apologetic look at Noah. "You said Liam was your kind of guy."

Thankfully, the child psychologist was seated at the other end of the table next to Mitzi. The pretty doctor was regaling that end of the table with a humorous story that had all those around her laughing uproariously.

Poppy's words corroborated what Liam had told him. Noah told himself he didn't care how Josie really felt. This *was* simply a game.

"I didn't know if Noah was interested in me at that point." Josie leaned over and laced her fingers with his. "Now I do."

Despite knowing that the touch was another prop, just a ploy to convince Ben and Poppy they were truly interested in each other, the sweet gesture eased Noah's tension.

"I didn't want to say I liked him when I had no idea if my feelings were reciprocated." Josie's smile turned rueful. "Especially since I'd always been so vocal about my determination never to get involved with a doctor."

Poppy laughed and elbowed her husband. "Sound familiar?"

Ben chuckled. "Yes, it does."

Josie frowned. "I don't understand. What's the joke?"

"My first husband was a neurosurgeon." Poppy slanted a quick glance at Noah. "He was arrogant and determined to run the show in his professional *and* private life. It's easy for doctors, especially surgeons, to think they know it all. When I came to Jackson Hole, I was determined not to date a doctor, especially a specialist. Then, my path crossed with Ben."

Ben's lips lifted in a smile. "She couldn't resist me."

Poppy laughed. "I did my best."

"She was not an easy woman to convince." Ben looped

his arm around his wife and pulled her close. "For a while, all signs indicated she preferred Groucho to me."

Noah lifted a brow. "Isn't Groucho your Schnauzer?"

"That's the one." Ben chuckled.

"The point is," Poppy's loving gaze settled on her husband, "the heart knows what it wants. Despite my initial fears and reservations, mine wanted you."

Though it wasn't something he and Ben had ever discussed, it was apparent to Noah that his partner loved his wife. Until this moment he hadn't realized how much.

"I want you to be happy, Josie." Ben jerked a thumb in Noah's direction. "If Anson does it for you, it's okay with me."

"Like I said, it's early days yet." Josie's eyes were suspiciously moist. "For now, it works."

Chapter Nine

Josie wasn't certain how she'd survived breakfast. Somehow she managed to eat yogurt, laugh and talk with those around her. Finally someone—Josie wasn't exactly sure who—announced it was time to pick up the children. Chairs were pushed back, money for the tip tossed in the center of the table and hugs exchanged between the women.

By the time she and Noah left, Josie's emotions were in such a tangle that the last thing she felt like doing was talking. But Noah reminded her on the way to the Land Rover that it was best to go over the encounter with her brother while it was still fresh.

She agreed to take the time, with the caveat she had to be back to get ready for her two o'clock yoga class.

Noah drove to the Elk Refuge just east of downtown Jackson. Though Josie couldn't imagine that many tourists would be interested in exploring the refuge the day after a snowfall, last night's snowfall had already been cleared from the empty graveled lot.

The sun shone bright through the windows of the Land Rover, warming the interior. Once they were parked, Josie released her seat belt and turned to face Noah.

"I was surprised to see you at the Coffee Pot."

"I reconsidered. You would be there with your brother." Noah's tone was matter-of-fact. "I'd made a commitment to help you with that relationship."

He'd come out of a sense of duty.

Josie couldn't figure out why the realization troubled her. "That still doesn't explain why you initially turned down the invitation."

He shrugged. "I'm not a big fan of these breakfast get-togethers. I was concerned you'd feel out of place as a single among so many couples. Of course, once I saw Liam, I realized you'd have been fine."

There was a watchful waiting in his eyes she didn't understand any more than she understood her sudden need to soothe. Josie chose her words carefully as if she was picking her way through a mine field. "I'm glad you decided to come."

Though he gave a brisk nod, she saw his shoulders relax.

"Tell me your thoughts on what was said," he demanded.

Straight to business, she thought, a little miffed. But then she remembered she was the one who'd made it clear she had limited time.

"It surprised me that Poppy originally had reservations about Benedict." Josie hadn't been around when her brother was dating his wife but they always seemed so happy she'd assumed their relationship had been smooth sailing from the beginning.

Noah waved aside the comment. "I don't see that as being relevant to our discussion."

Josie thought it might be, but wasn't sure how.

"I don't want to see you put yourself down again." His gaze met hers. "No matter what the reason."

"I—"

"No matter what the reason," he repeated.

Josie sighed. "At least it ended up serving a purpose."

Noah inclined his head. "What purpose would that be?"

"It made Ben think." Josie still couldn't believe her arrogant "I'm always right" brother had apologized. "You made him rethink his words and behavior. In the process you helped him see me in a way I never could have on my own."

"I'd like to take credit, but I believe that it was you standing up for yourself, calling Ben on his behavior, that made the difference."

"My brother is a stubborn guy."

"Ben is confident. He's decisive." Noah paused for a moment. "His wife was right. It's easy for physicians to believe they have all the answers. Patients look to them for guidance. Staff look to them for direction."

It was as close as Noah had ever come to admitting he could be arrogant. Sitting at the table earlier Josie had felt a connection with him. She experienced that same connection now, only stronger.

Josie knew she should have been pleased they'd come to an understanding of sorts and were working well together.

Instead, the realization scared her to death. Despite her reservations and the roadblocks she'd put up, one thing had become clear today.

She *liked* Dr. Noah Anson.

The next two weeks passed quickly. Noah put in long hours at the clinic and in the OR. Any free time, he spent with Josie.

Her yoga classes at the church were filling up as people put their New Year's resolutions into action. Though his grandmother continued to keep her busy running errands, Josie still managed to find time to scout out possible locations for her massage table.

Several independents offered her space but Josie said the "vibe" wasn't right and would keep looking. Noah suggested she speak with Meg Lassiter, who, along with several other physical and occupational therapists, owned a multispecialty clinic. Perhaps they would be interested in adding massage therapy to their growing list of available services.

While Body Harmony Inc. had only been in business for several years, it had built up a good referral base. It drew clients not only from the doctors located in Jackson Hole and nearby communities but also from word-of-mouth referrals.

Noah tapped the silver pen against the desk, tempted to call Meg and put in a good word for Josie. His practice sent a lot of business in Body Harmony's direction. And Josie wasn't just some random therapist off the street, she was John's daughter, Ben's sister and Noah's…friend.

If he called, would he need to tell Josie? She could see his intervention as interference.

The tapping became a staccato beat.

Josie would love working with Meg and all the other therapists. Noah had no doubt they'd love working with her. Still, what one person might see as helpful, another person might consider meddling. He continued to tap the silver Mont Blanc against the shiny desktop.

"Dr. Anson."

Noah stopped midtap as his nurse Charlotte stepped into his office.

"The Robidoux family is in the conference room."

"I'll be right there." Noah dropped the pen and shifted his focus to the medical folder on his desktop. A feeling of dread took up residence in the pit of his stomach.

The family, along with their daughter Cecelia, had traveled over a hundred miles today in search of hope.

Cecelia was twenty-six, the same age as Daffodil. She'd been referred by her oncologist in Idaho City. The type of brain tumor she'd had was deemed inoperable by the neurosurgeons she and her family had previously consulted.

Unfortunately, after reviewing the records, Noah had to concur with the assessment.

He didn't look forward to quashing the hopes of parents facing the death of their only child. Neither did he want to look into the eyes of a woman who should have so much life in front of her and admit he couldn't help her.

Sometimes being a doctor sucked, Noah thought as he rose to his feet and picked up the file.

The visit with Cecelia Robidoux, her family and her fiancé went as poorly as Noah had predicted. Still edgy and angry at life's injustices, Noah stopped on his way home to pick up a bottle of wine for dinner.

In the store, he ran into his sister. The interaction didn't go well.

Noah was still fuming thirty minutes later when he pulled into his driveway. Between the emotion-filled meeting with the Robidoux family and the encounter with Daffodil, Noah was in no mood for company.

Though he'd tried several times to call Josie to reschedule their meeting, each time he was sent straight to voice mail. That meant either she'd turned off her phone or, more than likely, had forgotten to charge it again.

He hoped she'd forgotten about their strategy session.

But when the garage door lifted, her car sat inside. He eased his vehicle next to hers, determined to make it an early night.

After eating they could briefly discuss strategies, then reschedule a more lengthy discussion for another time.

Noah simply stood for a minute in the garage. He wasn't sure if the overwhelming fatigue that wrapped around him like a shroud was due to the long morning surgery that had started at 6:00 a.m., the consultation with the Robidoux family or his altercation with Daffodil.

Probably a bit of all three, he decided.

The first thing Noah heard when he stepped into the house was Josie singing along to a rock classic. Her slightly off-key rendition brought a smile to his lips.

The scent of roasted chicken, and some other equally delicious aromas he couldn't recognize, filled the air. He drew in a deep breath and let some of the tension ease from his shoulders.

Noah hung his coat on a porcelain hook in the laundry room. He thought about calling out to announce his arrival but between the music and the way Josie belted out the words, she'd never hear him. Instead Noah leaned against the doorjamb and watched her chop carrots then toss them into a pot of boiling water on the stovetop. She was shoe-less with thick woolen socks on her feet.

She'd dressed casually for their dinner meeting in what he recognized as yoga pants coupled with a long-sleeved cotton shirt with script across the front. He wasn't close enough to decipher the words. Her hair had been pulled back from her face in a loose tail.

She looked completely at home. For some reason, that made him smile.

He admired her quick, efficient movements as she went about preparing the meal. From the table that was already set, it appeared they were eating in the kitchen, which was okay with him. As far as he was concerned, strategic planning didn't need to be stiff and formal.

After the day he'd had, relaxed and comfortable sounded just fine.

Noah waited until Josie put the knife down and stepped away from the boiling water before crossing to her. When he placed a hand on her shoulder, she gasped.

Reaching around her, he stilled the music, blaring from the iPad. "I didn't mean to startle you."

"You did, but that's okay." She gave a good-humored shrug. "The song is a favorite. I can get a little enthusiastic when I hear it. How was—" She paused, scanned his face. Concern filled her blue eyes. "What's wrong?"

"Long day." Avoiding her gaze, he moved to the counter where a bottle of wine sat breathing and lifted it. "Would you like a glass?"

"I'd love one. But only if you'll join me."

"I better pass." Noah placed the bottle back on the counter. "The way I feel right now, one glass would put me under the table."

Her eyes softened. "Ditch the tie and loosen your collar. We'll sit on the sofa and you can tell me about your day."

"You're busy." His protest fell on deaf ears. She was already pushing him into the other room.

The warmth of the fire Josie must have started coupled with the delicious aromas wafting from the kitchen wrapped around him like a favorite coat. But he couldn't sit on the sofa like a slug, not when there was so much to do. He thought of the pots on the stovetop. "I'll help you finish the meal."

Josie waved away the offer. "That's under control."

When he opened his mouth, she shook her head. "Your job is to remove that noose from around your neck. While you're at it, unfasten that top shirt button. And ditch the Italian loafers."

Noah inclined his head. "Bossy much?"

There was no heat or censure in the words. The woman was a born nurturer and simply doing what came naturally.

Josie tossed her head, making her ponytail swing from side to side like a pendulum. "I'm always bossy. And I'm bringing you a glass of wine, whether you want one or not."

When she left the room, Noah tugged off the tie and loosened his shirt collar. Because that felt so good, he slipped off his shoes. Then, because it was there, he propped his feet on the leather hassock.

He was reaching for the newspaper when she bustled into the room with a tray containing two wineglasses and a plate of antipasto. Noah jumped to his feet. "Let me help you."

He placed the tray on the coffee table in front of the sofa. Noah waited for her to sit, then sat beside her.

While they sipped their wine and munched on sweet pickles and olives, Josie told him what was on tap for dinner: rosemary chicken and new red potatoes, mixed green salad and baking powder biscuits. Coffee and crème brûlée for dessert.

It was a veritable feast. "Sounds delicious. Correction." He sniffed the air. "Smells delicious."

"We'll eat in thirty." She scooped up several roasted almonds. "More than enough time for you to fill me in on your day."

"Trust me." The sense of overwhelming weariness returned as he gazed into the fire. "You don't want to hear about it."

"Oh, but I do." Her voice was soft as melted butter. "You'll feel better if you talk about it."

The determined glint in those green eyes told him she

wouldn't give up until she'd pried every last bit of information out of him.

He took another sip of wine and considered where to begin. He started with the surgery. Although protracted and complex, he'd been pleased with the outcome.

"Seven hours," Josie murmured. "That's a long time on your feet. Not to mention a heckuva long time to stay on task."

"It was the highlight of the day. It was all downhill from there." Noah thought of the fear and despair on Cecelia Robidoux's face.

"Tell me." Josie's voice, soft and low, invited confidences.

He shifted and met her sympathetic gaze. They were business partners, nothing more. Then why did he feel so close to her now? Why did he feel as if he could tell her anything and she'd understand?

"Unlike the surgery, this story doesn't have a happy ending."

"Tell me," she repeated and so he did.

When he finished, making sure not to mention names, a sheen of tears glimmered in her eyes.

"There isn't anything you can do?" she asked. "Any hope you can offer the woman?"

"The tumor is wrapped around her brain stem."

There was no need to say more. Josie was not only a doctor's daughter, her father and brother were surgeons.

"Telling her there was nothing you could do had to have been horrible."

"All part of the job." The matter-of-fact delivery didn't ease the tension gripping his chest.

She met his gaze. "That doesn't make it easier."

"You're right." He drained the last of the wine from his

glass. "Other than the platitude that we never know what life holds, I could offer no hope."

There was a huskiness to his voice that hadn't been there only moments before. Embarrassed, Noah cleared his throat.

Inexplicably jittery, he'd have risen, except Josie chose that moment to slide close and slip her arm through his. She leaned her head against his shoulder and snuggled close.

The open display of affection amazed him. Though his grandmother had always been the hugging kind, his parents had been more hands-off.

Their behavior had been hardest on Daffodil, who'd always been more emotional and needy when it came to a comforting touch.

He'd done his best, letting her cry on his shoulder, listening instead of simply dismissing her childish concerns.

Noah saw now that, somewhere along the way, he'd stopped comforting, stopped listening. Somewhere along the way, he'd changed.

"I became my father," he murmured.

Thankfully Josie didn't appear to hear.

"What else happened today?" Josie's fingers absently toyed with the buttons on his shirtfront.

"My sister." He expelled a heavy breath. "I ran into her at the wine shop on the way here."

Her fingers stilled. "How did that go?"

"Not good." The irritation was back and with it the knowledge he'd somehow fallen short. That was a feeling he didn't like, not in the least.

"Did you two speak?"

The apprehension in her voice sparked his irritation.

"Of course I spoke to her." His voice snapped. "A conversation, I might mention, that *I* was forced to initiate because she strode past me as if I didn't exist."

Noah gritted his lips together as he recalled the encounter.

"What did Daffy say when you, ah, spoke to her?"

As if anticipating a problematic response, Josie straightened.

Noah discovered he missed the closeness. A fact that only irritated him further. Still, he kept a tight rein on his emotions. None of this was Josie's fault. "She denied seeing me."

"Any chance she was telling the truth?" Josie offered up the question in a matter-of fact tone.

"No." His tone was flat and hard.

For a second, something he'd seen in his sister's eyes had made him wonder if perhaps she *had* been preoccupied and hadn't noticed him. But the disdain in Daffodil's voice had been clear and confirmed the snub had been deliberate.

"Answer one question for me." She took a sip of wine, then held the stem loosely between her fingers rotating it forward and back. "What purpose could there be in ignoring you?"

He met her gaze. "General malevolence?"

Josie carefully placed her glass on the coffee table. Her expression turned serious. "I'm aware of the tension between you and Daffy. But your sister has never struck me as the mean-spirited sort."

"People can surprise you." He swiped a dismissive hand in the air. "Maybe she was having a bad day and decided to take it out on me."

"Or perhaps—" Josie paused for several beats, as her gaze swept over his face "—you'd had a bad day and took it out on her."

"Figures you'd take her side." The knowledge that

Josie's loyalties might rest with his sister was a bitter pill to swallow.

"This isn't about taking sides." Her voice was low and as soothing as the hand that now stroked his arm. "It's about reciprocating."

He lifted both brows.

"The other night you helped me see that I shouldn't press my father. The timing wasn't right." She lifted her shoulders, let them drop. "I'm merely suggesting your bummer of a day may have had you reacting more strongly than normal. Is that possible?"

After a moment's consideration, Noah gave a grudging nod. "Anything is possible."

"You and I have more in common than I first realized." There was a note of surprised wonder in her voice.

The fact that she appeared to be on his side after all piqued Noah's curiosity. "How do you figure?"

"When it comes to family, we both have a tendency to react in haste, repent in leisure." She smiled impishly. "Would you say that is a correct statement, Dr. Anson?"

There was something about that smile and the way she'd lumped them together in their dysfunctionality that had him nodding. "True enough."

She nodded in satisfaction and stood, holding out a hand to him. "Accepting our mutual shortcomings is a good start. Let's eat. Then we can formulate our strategy."

Though Noah didn't need any assistance, he took her hand, wanting the connection.

"We'll make it to the finish line," Josie predicted. "The grand prize will be family unity."

Noah wasn't a patient man. Not when it came to his personal life. He was a guy focused on end results.

But staring into Josie's clear green eyes, Noah had the feeling he was going to enjoy this journey every bit as much as crossing the finish line.

Chapter Ten

There was no decision to make. When Josie's mother called to ask her to dinner Wednesday night and mentioned her father was going to invite Noah—because wouldn't it be nice to include him?—Josie said she'd be there.

Accepting a dinner invitation with either one of their families was number three on the list arising from their strategy session the other night. While Noah could be a bit intense at times, Josie couldn't deny this was one ball he was determined to get rolling.

She pulled a cowl-necked sweater dress in hunter green from her closet, held it out in front of the mirror, frowned, then put it back.

Noah was determined to make progress every week, if not every day. While she wanted to mend fences with her family, she was in no hurry. Moving forward at a leisurely pace would have suited her just fine.

She understood Noah's need to see progress. While she'd just returned, he'd been trying for over a year and hadn't made a dent in Daffodil's armor. Josie shifted her attention back to her closet.

A blue jersey wrap dress held possibilities. She tossed it on the bed.

Next she selected a red cashmere sweater that would go nicely with the skirt she'd purchased last week. If she chose this outfit her mother would most definitely be pleased. She'd always loved seeing Josie in red.

Josie paused for a moment, soft fabric in hand, and realized her mother had often been complimentary. But over the years, her soft voice and supportive hugs had been drowned out by her father's "constructive feedback" and steely-eyed critical gaze.

A pretty melody briefly filled the air only to be repeated seconds later. She checked her phone and read the text. Noah had arrived.

Slipping on the sweater along with a tartan pencil skirt and black boots, Josie slipped a sparkly band in her hair, added some "kissable red" to her lips and headed downstairs.

Noah sat in the parlor with his grandmother and sister. He wore a charcoal topcoat over his suit and sat on the edge of the parlor chair. As he'd had to stop by the hospital before picking her up, they were running late.

She grabbed her jacket from the coat tree in the foyer, then stepped into the room. "I'm ready if you are."

Noah immediately stood. "You look lovely this evening."

A flush of pleasure heated Josie's cheeks. "Why, thank you."

Pauline rose. "Noah was just telling Daffodil and me about your father's plans to expand the clinic. Sounds as if they may be bringing in an additional neurosurgeon."

"First I've heard of it." She congratulated herself on

keeping the hurt from her voice. But she couldn't deny the sting.

How many times in the past had she learned about something going on with her own family from someone in the community? She shrugged aside the negative thought.

During their strategy session she and Noah had decided to focus on the future. *New beginnings* were their buzz-words going forward.

"Daffodil." Josie turned to the pretty hairstylist who sat sipping wine by the fire. "I've been meaning to tell you I've gotten a lot of compliments already on my new cara-mel highlights."

"They add a nice depth," Daffodil agreed. "I'm glad you're happy with them."

"Daff always did have artistic talent." Noah smiled at his sister. "The watercolor set you had when you were a little girl. You showed an eye for color even then."

Because Josie's eyes were on Daffy, she saw pleasure creep into the woman's eyes at the compliment.

"You gave me the watercolors for my birthday," Daffodil murmured.

"If I hadn't, you'd have probably scalped me." Noah chuckled and shifted his gaze to Josie. "It was the only thing on her list that year."

The grandmother's clock on the mantel chimed the hour.

"We need to scoot." Josie buttoned her coat and flashed a smile at Daffodil and Pauline. "Enjoy your evening."

"I'm sure we will." Pauline rose to walk them to the door.

"Goodbye, Josie." Daffodil's soft, melodic voice re-minded her of a harp being lightly plucked. "Have a nice evening, Noah."

He lifted his hand in farewell.

Josie waited until they were headed toward Spring Gulch to speak. "You handled that well."

His brows pulled together in obvious puzzlement. "Handled what?"

"Complimenting your sister, bringing up pleasant memories from the past." When she saw his continued confusion, she explained. "Those were two of the techniques we discussed."

"I wasn't consciously aware I was doing that." He frowned. "Her skill with color has been a lifelong thing."

"When was the last time you brought it up?"

He lifted a shoulder. "It's been a while."

"It's like what we discussed. Sometimes we only mention what we *don't* like about a person, not what we *do*. Our interactions stay focused on the negative. We forget they have good qualities. I don't know a person alive who doesn't like receiving a sincere compliment."

"You believe I'm making progress with Daff?"

The flash of hope she'd seen in his eyes tugged at her heart.

"Absolutely." Josie touched his coat sleeve. "I'm only sorry you couldn't stay and have dinner with her and Pauline."

"You and I had plans."

"I'm just saying tonight would have been a good opportunity for you and Daffodil to reconnect further."

"I'm not sure I agree."

Josie inclined her head. "Why not?"

"I don't want it to be that I show up every time she is with Gram." He shrugged. "That would keep her away for sure."

"I don't agree she'd stay away because of that, but I see your point." Josie suddenly pointed. "Look, a moose."

Noah slanted a glance toward the side of the road. As

large as a defensive linebacker, the moose was a muddy brown against a backdrop of white.

"I haven't seen one since I've been back." Josie laughed with delight. "Isn't he pretty?"

But it wasn't the animal that captivated Noah, it was the woman sitting beside him.

"The sparkle in your hairband matches the sparkle in your eyes," he heard himself say and nearly groaned.

Could he be any more lame?

But a quick grin told him she found the compliment pleasing. Then her lips twisted in a wry smile.

"I know what you're doing. Good job."

"What I'm doing?" He didn't have to feign confusion.

"Practicing giving compliments." She inclined her head. "It sounded sincere, too. That's really important."

"It *was* sincere." He found himself irritated. "I believe what we said is that compliments should be sincere. You were, in fact, the one who insisted that you can always find something nice to say about someone if you look hard enough."

"You're correct. Those are my words of wisdom."

"With you, I don't have to look hard to find something to like."

A look of startled surprise crossed her face. "Why, thank you, Noah. I can't recall the last time I received such a nice compliment."

They settled into a comfortable silence for the rest of the drive. Noah was glad that Josie was so relaxed. Especially when her mother excused herself after dinner to rest and her father ushered them into his study and shut the door.

"You may have noticed that your mother hasn't had as much energy lately." John Campbell's unsmiling gaze fixed on his daughter.

Beside him, Josie visibly stiffened.

"What's wrong with her?" Her voice sounded small and weak. She cleared her throat, tried again. "Why did she have to rest?"

Noah took her hand, reminding her he was here and she wasn't alone.

"I have the right to know the truth, Dad," Josie added when her father didn't answer.

Noah reached over and took her hand. He didn't think she even noticed.

"Last summer your mother began experiencing what she called an odd fluttering in her chest. After a series of tests, she was diagnosed with atrial fibrillation. She was put on medication." Her father rubbed his hands together. "We hoped the irregular rhythm would be controlled with medication."

"Was it?"

"Yes." John hesitated. "But your mother doesn't like the way the drugs make her feel."

Josie took another breath, then cleared her throat. "So what's the plan?"

Though her voice remained calm, Noah tightened his grip on her hand when it began to tremble.

"We considered several procedures to deal with the problem." John went on to say her mother had chosen to try cryoablation and that he agreed with her decision.

He took the next fifteen minutes to explain the procedure in detail and patiently answer his daughter's questions.

Tears filled Josie's eyes but she determinedly blinked them back.

"Lots of people have A-fib," Noah interjected. "Your mother will be fine."

"She will be fine," John repeated. "But she's worried

and lately has seemed a little…blue. I want to do something to lift her spirits."

Josie nodded. "What do you have in mind, Daddy?"

The startled look on John's face had Noah guessing it had been a long time since Josie had called him "Daddy."

John rose and began to pace the small room. "I don't know if you remember how your mother and I met."

"You met in junior high when her family moved to Colorado Springs, where you grew up," Josie said promptly. "It was love at first sight."

Noah sat back in the wing chair next to Josie's, content to sit and listen, her hand clasped in his.

"She was thirteen. I was fourteen." John's eyes took on a faraway look. "Your mother was the most beautiful girl I'd ever seen and so popular. She was way out of my science-geek league. Still, I couldn't help wanting her. She had this sweetness and joie de vivre…"

Noah saw Josie nod. Apparently all of this was old news.

"You're a lot like her, you know." John's gaze met his daughter's. "I see a lot of her in you. Always have."

Noah doubted John knew how much hearing that from him meant to Josie.

"By Christmas, we were going steady. Secretly, of course, because our parents would have thought we were too young for that kind of thing." His lips lifted, making the hard lines on his face soften. "That year, on Valentine's Day, I told her I loved her, that I would always love her. Then I gave her a heart necklace I'd purchased with my paper route money. It wasn't expensive, silver-plated with a few fake diamonds, but it made her happy."

"She still has it," Josie said softly. "She keeps it in her jewelry case."

Noah couldn't imagine making such a pledge at fourteen. Or having a popular girl like Josie give a serious guy like him the time of day.

"That was fifty years ago," John continued. "I'd like to surprise your mother and do something special to commemorate the occasion. I'd appreciate your help."

"Whatever you need," Josie promised.

"I was going to have Poppy help me," John added. "But with the morning sickness and running after Jack, I didn't want to add one more thing to her plate."

Josie deflated right before Noah's eyes.

Second choice.

Noah cursed John's insensitivity. Why had he felt the need to mention he'd considered asking Poppy? There had been no reason.

His admiration for Josie inched up a notch when she stiffened her shoulders and offered her father a smile.

"I'm happy to help." Josie met John's gaze. "Just tell me what you need."

He tapped a finger against his leg. "I was thinking a dinner party. Something small but elegant."

Noah wondered if his associate realized Valentine's Day was only two weeks away. Finding a venue to hold a celebration on such a popular day would be impossible.

That fact seemed to occur to Josie, as well. "Are you thinking of hosting the dinner party at your home?"

"Absolutely not." John looked startled. "I want this to be a surprise. It couldn't be if we held it here."

"We'll have to hold it at someone's home." Josie's brows furrowed in thought. "Ben and Poppy's would be a likely choice, but Poppy would insist on everything being perfect. With being pregnant, she doesn't need the additional stress."

John nodded his agreement.

"If you plan on inviting the doctors in your clinic, I

could ask Mitzi if we could have it at her house," Josie mused.

Before John could respond to that suggestion, Noah interrupted. "I have a better solution."

Two pair of eyes shifted to him.

"You can use my house."

"I couldn't ask you—" John began.

Noah lifted a hand silencing him. "Hear me out. Since Josie is planning the event, if it's at my place, she'll be able to come and go at will. Dori might be suspicious if she's invited to a Valentine event at Mitzi's home. But since Josie and I are dating she wouldn't think it at all strange to be invited to a party at my home."

Dating.

The word had rolled off Noah's tongue with an ease that left him stunned. The crazy part was it didn't feel strange at all to claim her as his girlfriend. It felt…right.

"It's a good solution." John slowly nodded. "If you're certain it's not an imposition."

"Not at all." Noah found he meant every word. "It will be a pleasure."

Josie walked out of her father's study with Noah at her side. Her head spun with everything that needed to be done in the next two weeks. She'd planned to ask Noah to take her straight home. Then, she saw her mother.

The bounce was back in Dori's step. Her mother appeared to have made the most of her brief respite, adding some color to her lips and running a brush through her stylish bob. Love welled up inside Josie.

It took every ounce of her self-control not to race across the room and enfold her mother in her arms. Instead, Josie painted a bright smile on her lips.

"Are you feeling better?" Thankfully her voice came out casual and offhand just as she'd intended.

"I am."

She looked it, Josie thought, more relaxed and not so pale.

Dori inclined her head. "What were you all doing in the study?"

The men exchanged a strained look.

Josie forced a laugh. "Dad was giving Noah the old 'you better be nice to my girl' lecture. I haven't heard that since I was in high school. It was a wonder I had any dates at all."

"I wanted those boys to know they needed to treat my daughter with respect or answer to me," John chimed in, playing along.

Dori smiled. "You were always so protective of your girl."

Josie had nearly forgotten about those fatherly "chats" her father had insisted on having with any of the guys she'd dated. Back then she'd groused about it, big time. Now she realized it was a sign he'd cared about her and her welfare.

"I assured John he didn't need to worry," Noah said, surprising her. "I would never hurt Josie."

John and Dori exchanged glances. The approval in her parents' eyes brought a flood of guilt.

"It's getting late. You're tired." Josie began to edge toward the front door.

Seeing the distress on her mother's face, Noah's hand tightened around Josie's fingers, holding her in place.

"Don't leave yet." Dori stepped toward her daughter, hands outstretched. "I thought we'd have coffee and look over some pictures."

"Pictures?" Between her father's news and the feel of Noah's palm against hers, Josie was having difficulty tracking.

Dori's gaze shifted to Noah. "I don't know about your mother but when my kids were growing up, we took lots of pictures. When Benedict brought Poppy home that first time, she had a grand time looking at his childhood photographs. Granted women tend to love that kind of thing more than men, but I think you'll enjoy seeing Josie in her cheerleading uniform."

Josie hated to disappoint her mother. Especially when she heard the hopeful note in her voice. But expecting Noah to look at old scrapbooks, well, that went beyond the call of duty.

She opened her mouth to politely decline but Noah spoke first.

"I'd love to see those photographs, Dori." He shifted his gaze to Josie and shot her a wink. "Afterward, maybe we can convince Josie to lead us in a cheer."

Chapter Eleven

"Josie can lead us in a cheer?" Josie's outraged tone ended in a chuckle. "I couldn't believe you said that…and I can't believe she made me do it."

"Go Broncs." Noah grinned. "Your mother enjoyed the evening."

That, Josie realized, was the point. She kept her voice easy, not wanting him to see just how much his kindness to her mother touched her. "You looked through those piles of scrapbooks because of her."

Noah pulled the Land Rover into his driveway and the garage door slid up.

"I agreed because I wanted to see a picture of you in your cheerleading outfit." He gave an exaggerated leer. "Or, even better, a bikini."

Josie's lips twitched. She could have insisted he take her home so she could research atrial fibrillation and the current strategies for treating it. She also needed to make a list of everything needing to be done to get the Valentine's party rolling.

A party that at least, thanks to Noah's generosity, had a venue. That he'd offered his home so readily was only one of the many things this evening that had confused her.

No, she wouldn't insist on going home. Not yet.

"Why did you tell my father we could have the party here?" she asked as the garage door slid closed, blocking out the snow and crisp night air.

He turned slightly in his seat to face her. "I thought that was obvious."

"Not to me."

"It assures me I'll be spending Valentine's Day with you."

"Are you flirting with me, Dr. Anson?"

"Perhaps I am." He smiled and her heart turned soft and warm.

Pondering the strangeness of the situation, Josie followed Noah into the house, unable to keep from noticing his stellar ass. Recalling how he'd acted only moments earlier, she gave an exaggerated leer at his backside, then had to stifle a giggle.

Noah abruptly turned and she offered him an innocent smile.

A suspicious gleam filled his eyes but he merely held out his hand for her coat.

Josie placed her jacket into the outstretched hand and trudged to the family room. An overstuffed sofa beckoned and she sank into its welcoming softness.

Noah got a fire going in the hearth then hesitated at the edge of the sofa. "May I get you something to drink?"

"A cup of hot tea would be nice."

He smiled. "Coming right up."

While he was gone she picked up a magazine on the

side table. It was a glossy spread of homes and condos in the Chicago area. A Realtor's card was clipped to the front with a website highlighted.

She flipped through the pages. The real estate prices seemed comparable to those in Jackson Hole.

He soon returned with the tea. The smile on his face dimmed when he saw what was in her lap.

She inclined her head. "Planning to relocate?"

Josie expected him to laugh and deny. Instead he removed the magazine from her lap. After placing it back on the side table, he handed her the tea then took a seat beside her on the sofa.

"There's no reason for me to stay in Jackson Hole if this last push to reunite with Daffodil doesn't work. In fact, my leaving might be easier on everyone. Gram is doing well. Daffodil seems content with her job and life here."

"You're just going to give up?" Josie couldn't keep the shock from her voice.

"I prefer to think of it as stepping back and giving her needed space." When Noah expelled a breath and raked a hand through his hair, she realized he wasn't as sure of his decision as he appeared.

Josie recalled what Daffodil had told her. "Didn't you try backing away once?"

Noah grimaced.

"It's true that after the wedding I left her and her new husband alone. But that was only after Daffy made it very clear she didn't want anything to do with me. I didn't want to cause trouble in her marriage, so yes, I took a step back."

Josie could only imagine how difficult that had been for him.

He jerked to his feet and began to pace. "After her divorce, I gave her some time to adjust, then I moved here to try to mend those fences. I thought she was ready. I'm not certain she is. This may be still too soon."

"You'll move if you don't make progress by March 1." Though she tried to stay calm, the words sounded like an accusation.

"I have a friend in Chicago. Edward is a brilliant neuro-surgeon. He's approached me about going into practice with him." Noah spoke in a brusque tone. "Though I won't leave right away, I need to give him my answer. If I do ac-cept his offer, I want to give your father and brother plenty of time to secure my replacement."

Noah might be leaving. A hard lump formed in the pit of Josie's stomach.

He resumed his seat beside her, casually resting his arm along the top of the sofa above her shoulders, and changed the subject. "Your mother having health issues surprised me."

"Today was the first I'd heard of it." Josie clasped her hands together. "She'll be okay. She's always been ex-tremely healthy."

His hand was now on her shoulder, a warm support that inexplicably made her feel better. He didn't spout plati-tudes that meant nothing, nor did he fill the silence with inane chatter.

Despite warning bells ringing loudly in her head, Josie rested her head against Noah's shoulder. They sat there for a long moment, the only sound their breathing and wood crackling in the hearth.

"For me, coming home was the right decision." She paused to still the tremor in her voice.

As she struggled to bring her rioting emotions under control, Noah stroked her arm with a reassurance that went beyond words.

"I was so angry at my father and brothers when I took

off. Not just because of the constant pressure to follow their dictates but from their attitude that if I didn't go along, I was stupid. My mother was never like that, but I was angry with her, too."

Instead of asking why, Noah continued to stroke her arm. When she shivered, he grabbed a cashmere throw with his free hand and tucked it around her.

"She didn't stand up for me, Noah." Her voice held a plaintive edge that she hated. "My mother may not have piled on the pressure like the rest of them, but she threw me to the wolves."

"You felt betrayed." There was no criticism in his voice. It was a simple statement of fact.

Josie briefly closed her eyes. When she opened them she had to blink away tears that had somehow appeared. "If only she'd supported me, let me know she understood my concerns. If she'd just been there for me."

He brushed a kiss against her hair and pulled her even closer.

"I honestly believe she thought she was being neutral," Josie said in answer to the question she'd expected him to ask. "But when you say nothing, it's as if you're siding with the majority. Sort of like if you don't vote, you're really siding with whoever wins."

Noah leaned over and kissed her. "You need to speak with her about your feelings."

"I know." She sighed. "But how can I do it now, when she has these heart issues?"

"You'll know when the time is right."

She wished he'd kiss her again. "Do you really think so?"

"You're a smart, sensitive woman. You read people well." He tucked a strand of hair behind her ear. The gentle brush of his fingers was somehow erotic. "You'll pick the opportune time."

"You sound surprised."

"I suppose in a way, I am." Noah shook his head, chuckled. "I've been guilty of equating pretty and vivacious with little to no substance."

She gazed at him through lowered lashes. "How very shortsighted of you."

"I never claimed to be perfect." He tugged her so close she was practically sitting on his lap.

"I won't hold your lack of perfection against you." Even as her heart fluttered, she kept her tone deliberately light. Lordy, he smelled good. "I'm not perfect, either."

Noah slid a strand of her hair between his thumb and forefinger, his gaze never leaving her face. "From where I'm sitting, you look pretty near perfect."

His words, his look, had her heart turning to a lovely, warm mass in her chest.

"Are you sure you don't want to turn on a lamp?" But she didn't need additional wattage to detect the passion simmering in his blue depths.

Red, warning lights pulsed. Kissing Noah, having sex with Dr. Anson, hadn't been on tonight's agenda. But she couldn't deny she wanted him.

What was a woman to do?

Take control, Josie thought. *Make my own decisions.*

Wasn't that what she'd needed to do all along?

While she was making her own decisions, he began to nuzzle her neck.

"Intimacy wasn't part of the deal," she sputtered as a hot riff of sensation traveled up her spine.

Noah trailed a tongue behind her ear making her entire body quiver before lifting his head. "What's happening right now doesn't have a thing to do with our agreement."

"What does it have to do with?"

"How hot you looked in that cheerleading outfit," he said and made her laugh.

His gaze grew solemn, his eyes a deep, fathomless blue. "Stay the night."

"I have to work for your grandmother in the morning."

"I have appointments beginning at eight," he countered, then sat back and gave her space.

Good old-fashioned common sense said she needed to maintain a distance. But hadn't her return to Jackson Hole been about following her heart?

Closing the distance he'd just put between them seconds before, she pressed her mouth to his lips. Then, she began unbuttoning his perfectly starched shirt.

His hands settled on her shoulders, the touch scorching her all the way through the fabric of her sweater. "What are you doing?"

Her fingers paused for only a second. "Getting you naked, of course."

A slight smile lifted the corners of his lips. "What about the debriefing?"

"Later." Four buttons down. An unknown number to go. She could have counted but not with him scattering kisses on her face and neck. Counting, Josie decided, suddenly seemed vastly overrated.

He took the lobe of her ear between his teeth and nibbled.

Emotions swirled inside her filling her to bursting.

"Yes." Josie arched her neck back as he trailed kisses down her throat. "Oh, yes."

"Just the words I've longed to hear," he said in a theatrical baritone.

Her chuckle was swallowed up by his mouth capturing hers in a soul-scorching kiss that left her gasping. He continued to kiss her, alternating long, dreamy kisses with the more erotic varieties. It wasn't long before her head spun and her mind turned to mush.

What little control remained nearly shattered when he slid his hand under her sweater and deftly unclasped her bra. He cupped one breast high in his hand, circling the peak with his fingers.

Somewhere in her lust-induced haze she realized he'd pulled her sweater over her head. That was fine with her. The man had clever hands. When his mouth took over, Josie gasped and slid her fingers in his hair.

The warmth in her lower belly turned fiery hot and became a pulsating need.

But when his hand slid under her skirt, her brain finally awakened. She clamped her fingers around his wrist. "Do you have protection?"

It wasn't the most romantic of questions but she wasn't totally out of control. Not yet.

His eyes burned in the charged atmosphere. He nodded. "Upstairs."

"Get one. Get a few. Bring the whole box." Her pulse was a swift, tripping beat. She fought to get her breath under control. "I'll wait."

"If you're too warm." He shot a pointed glance at her skirt and boots. "You could use the time to take those off."

"You're so helpful," she said but he was already sprinting down the hall.

Josie smiled and unzipped her boots. She supposed she could use this time to think about what she was about to do, but what was there to think about?

She wanted to have sex with Noah.

He wanted to have sex with her.

She wasn't ready to call what they were about to do "making love" because love didn't have anything to do with what was about to occur on this sofa. It was pure physical need and she hoped the release would ease the simmering tension that filled the air whenever they were in the same room. The second boot had just dropped to the floor when Noah returned.

He stopped short of the sofa, mere inches away, and simply stared.

The moment her eyes touched his, something inside her seemed to lock into place and she could not look away.

Determined not to be embarrassed by her nakedness, she smiled sweetly. "I took your suggestion."

He stopped, cleared his throat. "What suggestion would that have been?"

"That I remove the rest of my clothes."

With a suspiciously easy grin he kissed the base of her jaw. "Appreciate the follow-through."

She opened her arms to him and smiled. "Join me on the sofa."

She didn't have to ask twice.

Noah stripped off his clothes and flung them aside. He walked toward her wearing only black silk boxers.

Josie let her gaze linger on his lean, athletic form. "I'd have pegged you for a briefs man."

He looked so affronted she had to laugh. Noah might appear starched and arrogant on the outside, but she was growing to like him. Not enough to date him but definitely enough to sleep with him.

"You're so beautiful." He knelt by the sofa and slid a hand down her belly, stopping just short of her thatch of blond curls. "Your skin is like porcelain, smooth and flawless."

She shivered as he played with her curls then slowly moved his hand up to her breast. He trailed a finger around and around, stopping just short of the nipple.

Josie's body responded with breathtaking speed, a sensation she didn't bother to fight.

At last, Noah skimmed the edge of a short-cropped nail over the tip, making her gasp.

She nipped his neck—her own version of foreplay—and Noah jumped. Then he laughed in delight and began scattering his own version of love bites down her body until he reached the area he sought.

"Spread your legs." It might have been an order except for the soft caress in his voice.

Though she complied, he nudged them even farther apart with his knee. Then he bent down, his tongue dipping inside her heated core.

Josie gasped and fisted her hands in the cashmere throw and bucked up. In and out his tongue slipped, stoking the fires that now burned out of control. Then his mouth found the single spot of pleasure and he began to suckle, easy at first, then with a rhythm that drove her to madness.

She thrashed from side to side and fisted her hands in his hair, crying out as her need grew. She tried to catch her breath then gave up on air as her release claimed her.

Her climax rippled through her and still he touched her, gentling the contact until the last drop had been wrung from her body.

She had a second to relax, to cuddle beside him sated and drowsy, feeling as if all was right in the world. Then he began to kiss her again, to caress her body with hands that had so quickly discovered where she liked to be touched.

Her desire bloomed again. Through half-shut eyes, she gazed at his muscular physique, at the corded muscles, the flat abdomen and his arousal.

"Impressive," she said and made him smile.

He unwrapped the condom, but when he began to pull it on, she removed it from his fingers, brushing aside his hand.

"Let me." She planted a kiss against his belly just above where the erection reached.

"Not playing fair," he groaned.

"I'm not a by-the-rules kind of gal." She rolled the condom over the silky head and down the shaft. She turned and gazed up at him. "Looks like someone is ready to come in and play."

When he pressed his body against her, the heat of him punched into her like a blazing furnace. She longed to once again run her hands over his body, to feel the coiled strength of skin and muscle sliding under her fingers. She wanted him to touch her in the same way, wanted to feel the weight of his body on hers. Wanted to feel him inside her.

Noah settled between her legs and kissed her breasts. She felt a shivery kind of ache all over. Her heart hammered so loudly the only thing she heard was a whooshing sound in her ears.

She rubbed against his erection. The flames of desire she'd thought fully sated only moments before, burned out of control. She nipped his ear. "Inside me, Noah. Now."

Josie wasn't sure if it was saying his name or if he simply couldn't wait any longer either, but he eased inside her.

He was large and stretched her in the best way possible. She felt filled, yet the need for more grew.

Noah wrapped his arms around her, drawing her close so they pressed together everywhere. He took it slow, pushing in then moving out.

Impatient, and filled with a need that only he could quench, Josie urged him deeper.

"More," she demanded as he withdrew only to fill her again.

"Patience," he murmured, taking her mouth in a long kiss before plunging deeper.

She moaned at the sensation and wiggled in an attempt to ease the rising pressure.

"No. Don't move like that... I can't...you need more—"

"I need you." She pressed against him. "All of you. Now."

With a groan, Noah thrust and plunged all the way in, burying himself inside her.

Josie gasped.

He remained absolutely still for a heartbeat. "Are you okay?"

She gave a jerky nod.

"I'll pull out."

But when he moved, the brief pain she'd experienced was replaced by a shiver of need that ran all the way to the tips of her toes.

She put her hands on his taut biceps and squeezed. "Come back to me."

His gaze searched her eyes. "Are you sure?"

Her answer was a moan of pleasure.

Taking it slowly, he began to move inside her, in and out, in and out.

Gentle thrusts at first, then more forceful. Josie wrapped her legs around him, holding him tight. He continued to kiss her, his tongue delving inside her mouth even as his thick erection filled her.

He consumed every part of her. She couldn't focus on anything but him and how he made her feel. Then her body convulsed in release once again and she could only hang on as he took her to heaven and back.

When Noah was certain he couldn't give her any more pleasure, he gave one final thrust, shuddered in her embrace and called out her name.

Chapter Twelve

Josie didn't spend the night. Though Noah wanted her to stay, she insisted he drive her home, saying she didn't want Pauline to get the wrong idea about their relationship.

When he asked what wrong idea that might be, she'd told him quite seriously that she preferred his grandmother didn't think they were "too involved." It was one thing for everyone to believe they were dating but she wanted to keep the fact they were sleeping together quiet.

Though Noah had always been one to protect his privacy, her desire for secrecy troubled him.

The next morning Noah woke early. This gave him time for breakfast before heading to the clinic. In no particular rush, Noah sipped his coffee, then pulled on his shoes. He took a moment to consider the previous evening.

If he was being honest he'd say that he wasn't surprised he and Josie had ended up having sex.

Over the past few weeks, he'd grown increasingly aware—and fond—of her. He admired her determination to fix things with her family. Though the sexual tension between them had never been a topic of discussion, he knew she'd wrestled with the attraction as much as he had…

Last night, they'd made a conscious decision to act on that attraction. It had been obvious she'd enjoyed the experience. He'd been with other women, but last night had been…different, better. Still, Noah wasn't convinced it'd be wise for them to continue the intimacy.

If he didn't reconcile with his sister before March 1, he'd be leaving Jackson Hole.

Building a relationship with Josie wouldn't be wise.

Noah told himself he'd simply push all thoughts of the closeness and the heat they'd shared from his mind.

He wouldn't think of it again.

Josie had to stop herself from humming as she slipped out of the dress shop in downtown Jackson. The sun shone bright in the sky and the only thing on her agenda this morning was running errands for Pauline.

Once she'd returned home last night, she'd slept like the dead. Thankfully, Pauline had already retired for the evening so she didn't have to explain her disheveled appearance.

Not to mention explain why she was arriving home at such a late—or rather early—hour. She really needed to get her own place. While the rent Pauline charged was minimal, Josie didn't like feeling as if she was a teenager sneaking in after curfew.

What if the weather was bad next time? Or she simply decided she wanted to sleep over? She didn't want Pauline to fret but neither did she want to have to check in with an employer, a boss who also happened to be Noah's grandmother.

Right after Valentine's Day, Josie would begin her apartment search.

She'd almost reached her car when she caught sight of a familiar figure halfway down the block going into Perfect Pizza. Josie quickened her steps. Sylvie Thorne was just the woman she wanted to speak with today.

By the time Josie reached the popular pizza place, Sylvie had already ordered, picked up her drink and was on her way to the adjacent dining area.

"Sylvie," Josie called out. "Hello."

The Mad Batter owner turned and flashed a bright smile. "Hi, Josie. Are you here for lunch, too?"

"I am." It wasn't exactly the truth, but it sounded better than saying she'd followed Sylvie inside the restaurant.

Josie glanced at the board where the pizza toppings were listed, along with the pizza of the day, which appeared to be cream cheese and pineapple.

"I ordered a medium special-of-the-day." Sylvie moved to her side as Josie studied the offerings. "If you'd like to share, there will be plenty. Unless you have your heart set on another topping."

"Actually I've been dying to try the cream cheese and pineapple, so if you're sure you don't mind sharing…"

"I'd love to have you join me."

"I'll pay you—"

"Don't worry about it." Sylvie surveyed the utilitarian dining area with its knotty pine booths and wooden tables. "How about a booth?"

"Sounds good to me." She followed Sylvie to one directly in front of a window facing the street.

Both women were dressed casually in jeans and boots topped with heavy woolen coats to keep out the frigid January wind. Once they'd slipped them off and hung them on the pegs on the side of the booth, Josie slipped into the bench opposite Sylvie.

Her new friend wore a dark cropped sweater with fur cuffs that Josie recognized as a Sally LaPointe.

"I love your sweater. The cuffs are very cool."

"It was a gift." A look of sadness filled Sylvie's eyes. "From someone very special to me."

"Your ex-fiancé?"

"No." Sylvie lifted the glass of tea to her lips. "From the woman who eventually married him."

"Whoa, hold the horses. What—"

Josie was prevented from asking all the questions poised on her lips when the server appeared with the pizza. Large chunks of pineapple artfully decorated the top of a golden-brown crust. The pie looked amazing and smelled delicious.

The server, a teenager with jet-black hair with a magenta streak, cut them each a slice and placed the pieces on plates.

"Are you sure you don't mind sharing?" Josie's mouth began to water at the sight of the delectable piece in front of her. "If this was mine, I'd want to keep it all to myself."

"I'm only one person." Sylvie laughed, a silver tinkling sound. "This is enough for at least five."

"Well, thank you." Instead of forking off a piece Josie leveled her gaze on Sylvie. "Tell me about the friend who gave you that gorgeous sweater."

"I will," Sylvie assured. "Not today."

"Oh, okay. I didn't mean to pry."

"You didn't."

But Josie knew she had so she shifted the conversation to a familiar standard, the weather. They spent the next several minutes eating pizza and talking about the weather and the all-important Jackson Hole snow reports and skiing conditions.

Since both of them were occasional skiers at best, the discussion didn't last long. Josie eyed another piece of pizza but she'd already wolfed down two large slices. Eating a third would be pure gluttony.

"How's the bakery business going?" Josie asked, keeping her tone casual.

"Picking up. Thanks to the cake I did for the New Year's Eve party and the one you took to the book club, I've garnered some additional business." Sylvie met her gaze. "Thank you. Your kind words and referrals are very much appreciated."

Josie felt embarrassed by the praise. "I really haven't done much. Unless you count gushing and raving about your fabulous skills and talent."

Sylvie laughed. "Well, whatever you're doing, keep it up. Cassidy Duggan stopped by this morning and ordered a cake for her twin daughters' birthday party."

"I'm glad things are going so well for you." Josie leaned forward, resting her forearms on the table. "I have another job for you. If you're interested, that is."

Sylvie wiped the corners of her lips with a paper napkin from the chrome dispenser on the table. "Of course I'm interested. Tell me about it."

"This will be well worth your time." Josie knew her father would spare no expense to make every aspect of this party the best.

Sylvie moved her pizza plate aside and leaned forward, resting her forearms on the table. "You've got my interest."

"It's for my mother." Josie spent the next few minutes explaining the situation about her mother and her father's desire to make this Valentine's Day extra special.

"That is so amazingly sweet." Sylvie's eyes turned

dreamy. "I don't know your father but he sounds like a very nice man."

"He has his moments," Josie said with a droll smile. Still, she couldn't deny that he loved his wife.

"What kind of cake are you looking for?"

"When my mother was regaling Noah with all my child-hood pictures, I pulled—"

"Hold it." Sylvie raised a hand. "A mother showing a guy your scrapbooks is serious stuff."

Josie chuckled. "Not if you know my mom. She uses any excuse to pull out the books."

Sylvie looked doubtful.

"Anyway, while she was plying Noah with photos, I pulled my father aside and asked what kind of cake he thought she'd like. Guess what he said?"

"Let me guess." Sylvie brought a finger to her lips and her eyes filled with an impish gleam. "A heart cake?"

"Ding, ding, ding." Josie laughed. "You win the prize. How'd you guess?"

"Your father is a surgeon. They're great at cutting, not so great at visualizing something unique." Sylvie's brows furrowed. "Does he have his mind set on a heart-shaped cake?"

Josie glanced around the dining area that was now full. Though she didn't recognize anyone within earshot, she lowered her voice. Jackson Hole wasn't that big and her parents were active in the community. "I suggested it might be nicer if we went a little more personal on the cake. He concurred."

Sylvie cocked her head. "Did he come up with any ideas?"

"As a matter of fact, he did." Josie heaved a sigh of satisfaction. "It took a while—thank God for all those scrapbooks—but he reminded me how much my mom loves shoes."

"Perfect." Sylvie licked her lips in anticipation, or perhaps she was removing a spot of cream cheese. "I have some fabulous ideas on what we can do with that."

"I knew I could count on you." Josie tapped a finger against her lips. "Perhaps you could take a few days, maybe draw up some ideas and then we could discuss?"

"Will we need to find a time your father could meet with us?"

Josie shook her head. "I'm handling all the arrangements. He gave his input. Now it's up to me—and you—to run with it."

"You're a good daughter."

"I want to be," Josie said with a sigh. *Oh, how she wanted to be…*

"This will be a memorable occasion," Sylvie said with a confidence Josie found reassuring. "Do you have a venue for the party? Any idea how many will be in attendance?"

"I would say a guest list of ten or twelve. My father wants small and intimate." Josie wondered why she felt embarrassed to admit where the party would be held. "Noah offered his house."

"Did he?" Sylvie's tone gave nothing away. Neither did her expression.

"At this late date we weren't going to be able to secure a party room, not when my father insists on having the event on the fourteenth. We can't have it at his house because it's a surprise. My mother doesn't know anything about this and we want to keep it that way." Josie paused to take a breath.

"Good to know."

"Anyway, my brother's wife is pregnant and Dad didn't want to impose on her, so Noah volunteered," Josie added.

Sylvie's expression showed no emotion. She lifted her glass of tea and peered at Josie over the rim. "Noah must think a lot of you to open his home to your family."

"It's not like that," Josie hastened to clarify. "Noah is in practice with my father and is a friend of my brother."

"He's also your good friend," Sylvie pointed out.

"For now." As Sylvie had done earlier, Josie's tone made it clear that this subject was also closed.

Sylvie nodded and finished the last bite of pizza left on her plate. "If there's any way I can help you with the party, please let me know. You don't have much time to pull this together."

"A little over two weeks." Forgetting her earlier resolve to not eat any more, Josie gave in to temptation and reached for another slice of pizza. "I'm fairly organized so if I keep myself on task, I should be able to get it all done…as long as I don't waste time on frivolous details."

Josie stopped by Noah's house that evening for a tour, with the specific purpose of figuring out where everything would go.

He showed her around, keeping a respectful distance and making absolutely no move to touch her. For a few seconds she wondered if he'd somehow forgotten what happened between them last night. Or maybe it had simply been a deliciously erotic dream?

Only when she'd turned to the door to leave, had he spun her around and kissed her. One thing quickly led to another. Before she knew it, they were naked on his king-size bed, then naked in the shower.

Now here she sat, partially dressed, enjoying a late supper of grilled cheese sandwiches and fruit. The sliced grapefruit and orange pieces also seemed a necessity. She needed something to cut through the arteries likely clogged by an overabundance of cheese in one day.

Noah sat across the table, hair still damp from the shower. Instead of his normal suit and tie attire, he looked relaxed and more approachable in gym shorts and a faded blue T-shirt. She was even more casual, having pulled on one of his white shirts. She supposed she could have pulled on her jeans…and she planned to do just that…once she located her underwear. The lace panties were somewhere in the house. She just had to find them.

"Your father is really cranked about this party." Noah washed down a bite of thick bread and cheese with a big gulp of milk. "He was telling Ben and Mitzi all about it today."

"Does Mitzi know about my mom's A-fib?"

Noah paused, a slice of orange halfway to his mouth. "I don't believe so."

"He's worried." Josie swallowed hard. "So am I."

She couldn't believe she'd voiced the fear. In the years away Josie had gotten used to handling every crisis on her own. While she'd always had her friends' support, she realized now just how alone she'd felt.

Noah reached across the table and covered her hand with his. "She'll be fine."

Josie blinked back sudden tears and scolded herself for being such a baby.

Pull yourself together.

She straightened and when she spoke her voice was steady. "I did some research earlier today on the procedure. It's not a walk in the park."

"It's more of a walk than you might think, especially when performed by an experienced surgeon." Noah's voice reverberated with confidence. "Dr. Marvin—the doctor your parents chose for the procedure—was one of the first cardiologists in Wyoming to perform the procedure. Balloon cryoablation was approved by the FDA in late 2010."

"It sounds nasty." Josie wrinkled her nose.

He squeezed her fingers. "Trust me. While it isn't *a walk in the park*, it gets good results."

"I'm sorry." Josie stiffened her spine. "Whining about it doesn't help."

"Talking about it *can* help." Noah spoke with surprising gentleness. "If you ever want to discuss any part of the procedure, or anything else that is troubling you, I'm here. Or if you need a distraction…"

"I'd say lately you've been doing a stellar job of keeping me distracted."

Noah feigned confusion. "I don't know what you mean."

Josie snorted. "That innocent smile may fool your grandmother but it doesn't fool me. I'm the one sitting at your table wearing a shirt and no underwear."

"I'm not likely to forget that fact." His gaze dropped to her chest and her nipples turned to hard peaks.

"We should be strategizing, planning our next move." She tried to sound cross but couldn't quite pull it off. Not with blood flowing through her veins like warm honey and desire spurting like a fresh spring flower. "Instead, all we can think of is getting naked again."

"I find being without clothing clears my head and allows me to think more clearly."

She had to laugh.

"It's time for a little experiment." He dropped his half-eaten sandwich on the plate, pushed back his chair and rose, holding out his hand. "We'll go to the bedroom—"

"We've already done it once."

He inclined his head.

"Okay, twice, though I'm not sure a quickie against the shower wall counts."

"The way you were moaning." He shot her a wicked smile. "I'm pretty sure it counts."

She swatted his shoulder. "I wasn't the only one moaning."

"No. You weren't. I want you, Josie." His voice was a husky rasp as he captured her hand and pulled her to her feet. "If you're not interested, just tell me."

Josie kissed the hollow under his neck. "I am interested. I'm so interested it scares me. That probably doesn't make sense—"

"It does," he admitted. "Don't worry. It's been a while for both of us. We have this passion stored up and we're simply releasing it. Give us a couple more times and this will be under control."

She inclined her head. "You're saying that for now, the smartest course of action is to simply get this out of our system?"

"Exactly." His lips may have twitched but she couldn't be sure.

Josie wrapped her arms around Noah's neck and gave him a ferocious kiss. "Well then, what are we waiting for?"

Chapter Thirteen

On Friday, after her morning yoga class, Josie met with Sylvie at Hill of Beans to go over cake designs.

"This is it." Josie pointed to an image of a cake with pale pink frosting decorated with alternating hot-pink and black strips of fondant with shiny little black bows made out of sugar. The pièce de résistance was the shimmery black stiletto resting on the top. She leaned close. "Is that a real shoe?"

"Looks real, doesn't it?" Sylvie smiled. "It's made out of sugar."

"I love it. My mom will love it, too."

"It's a gorgeous cake and very unique," Sylvie admitted. "But I need to warn you. It's very labor-intensive, which makes it pricey."

"Cost isn't a concern. While my father appreciates getting a good deal as much as the next guy, he wants this occasion to be perfect."

"How long have they been married?"

"Nearly forty years." Josie shook her head. "Sounds like an eternity, doesn't it?"

Sylvie nodded. "They must be well-suited."

"They are," Josie grudgingly admitted.

She'd never given much thought to her parents' relationship. While they occasionally became angry with each other, they never stayed that way. Unlike many of her friends, as a child Josie had never worried about her parents separating or divorcing. They'd always seemed, well, so much in love.

The look in her father's eyes when he'd talked about her mother's upcoming procedure had clearly shown her that those emotions had only deepened through the years.

After concluding her conversation with Sylvie, Josie headed over to a local microbrewery, not far from the courthouse, for her appointment with Lexi Delacourt. Because Lexi worked full-time as a social worker for Teton County, they'd chosen a spot not far from her office for their late afternoon meeting.

Josie had just snagged a high-top table when Lexi texted she was running late. As it was happy hour with free chips and salsa and half-priced margaritas, Josie didn't mind the wait. It gave her a chance to review the various meal options Lexi had posted on her website.

She'd barely pulled up the menus and the pricing on her phone when Hailey Randall, an old friend from high school, stopped over to say hello and introduce Josie to her husband, Winn Ferris. She discovered Hailey was a speech therapist working at Body Harmony.

Which Josie decided just went to show—again—what a small world it was in Jackson Hole.

By the time Lexi slid onto the stool at the high-top table, Josie hadn't even glanced at the menus.

"I'm sorry I kept you waiting." Lexi shot her an apologetic look. "I had a placement that took longer than I anticipated."

"No worries." Josie waved away Lexi's apologies. "This gave me a chance to reconnect with a friend I hadn't seen in years. Hailey Randall, er, Ferris. Do you know her?"

"Of course, I know Hailey. She and her husband are friends of ours." Lexi waved to someone across the room. "That's what I love about Jackson Hole. There's so many wonderful people living here. It took my husband, Nick, a while to accept that fact. When we first got married, he really pushed for us to live in Dallas."

Josie took a sip of her lime margarita. "Why there?"

"Nick was from there. That's where the family's law practice is located." Lexi grabbed a chip, signaled the waiter and pointed to Josie's margarita before continuing her explanation. "Initially we agreed to six months here and the other half in Dallas. But his practice here has grown by leaps and bounds, we have kids in school now and all our couple friends are here. So, now we spend the majority of the year in Jackson Hole."

While they waited for the waiter to bring Lexi's drink, they munched on chips and chatted about mutual friends. When Josie mentioned to Lexi she was a massage therapist, Lexi's eyes lit up. She brought up her friend Meg Lassiter's multispecialty therapy clinic.

"Have you thought about contacting her?" Lexi paused to smile her thanks at the handsome young server who brought her drink and refilled the basket with more chips. "I think you'd be a great addition to the group."

Josie sipped her drink and grabbed a chip, keeping her disappointment firmly under wraps. "I called and asked if they'd ever thought of adding a massage therapist to their practice. The woman I spoke with told me not at this time."

Josie had thought about mentioning her interest to

Hailey—when she'd learned where her friend worked—but the time hadn't seemed right.

"That surprises me they wouldn't even schedule an interview to discuss the possibility." Lexi's dark brows pulled together. "Who did you speak with?"

"I'm not sure," Josie admitted.

"That response doesn't make sense." Still frowning, Lexi bit into a chip. "I'd like to mention you to Meg…if you don't mind."

"I don't want to be a bother…"

"Why would it be a bother? Either she'll be interested or not." Lexi took a hefty sip of her margarita and heaved a sigh of appreciation.

"If you want to call her, that'd be great. In the meantime, I'll reach out again." Josie munched thoughtfully on a chip. "I suppose following up after an initial 'no' is really no different than what I'm doing now, contacting you after you turned my dad down."

Lexi lifted a chip from the basket and Josie saw the puzzlement in her eyes. "Your father mentioned in passing some party on Valentine's Day. I didn't turn him down. I merely said that's always a busy time."

Josie's heart picked up speed. Had her father misunderstood? He'd made it sound as if she had no chance of securing Lexi's services.

"This isn't just any Valentine's party." Josie went on to explain the specifics. By the time she finished, Lexi had tears in her eyes. "That is so sweet. Of course I'll do it. I'd love to help them celebrate such a special occasion."

"Poppy and I can serve the food," Josie added, "so you could leave early. That way you and Nick can still celebrate Valentine's Day."

Lexi reached over and squeezed Josie's hand. "I'll stay as long as you need me."

"Like I said, we're only planning on six couples," Josie assured her. "Sylvie Thorne will handle the cake."

"Good choice." Lexi nodded her approval. "Her cakes are amazing."

A warm surge of satisfaction washed over Josie. The cake was covered. Now she had the best caterer in the Hole on board.

"Thanks so much for agreeing to do this, Lexi. Again, I apologize that it's so last minute. My father decided to do this last minute, once he knew when my mother's procedure would be."

"When is her procedure scheduled?"

"The sixteenth."

"If she wants to speak with someone who's had it done, I can put her in touch with Nick's dad." Lexi gave her a reassuring smile. "He had it done two years ago. Complete success."

"That's good to know. I'll mention it to my father. I'm not sure if I'm supposed to be saying anything—"

"I won't say anything about it unless you give me the go-ahead," Lexi assured her. "Now, let's talk options."

Josie's head spun with all the choices, each of which sounded wonderful. By the time the brunette rose to leave, they had the menu nailed down.

While Lexi was eager to get home to make dinner for her family, Pauline had her bridge group over and Josie was in no hurry to return home. She could stop by her parents' home but they'd likely be entertaining, something her mother enjoyed and did on a regular basis.

Josie ordered another margarita and made a call to Body Harmony, requesting Meg Lassiter return the call at her convenience. Then she pulled the iPad from her oversize bag. The sounds of the noisy bar drifted away as she made a list of everything she needed to accomplish before the party.

"Hey, pretty lady."

Her heart leaped at the sound of the masculine voice, but fell almost instantly when she realized it wasn't Noah.

She had to admit Liam Gallagher made an engaging sight in his dark brown pants and cream-colored sweater. But the sight of him didn't make her heart beat even the slightest bit faster.

He flashed an engaging smile. "Is this seat taken?"

Josie smiled. "It'll cost you."

He laughed and pulled out the chair Lexi had vacated only moments before. The server stopped by before he'd even sat down. Once he'd ordered, Liam grabbed a chip. "What's the price of a chair nowadays?"

"Har har." Josie sipped her margarita. "If you have any patients you feel would benefit from yoga or massage, I'd like you to send them my way."

"I can do that." Liam's beer appeared and he paid the server for not only his drink but picked up Josie's tab, as well. He waved aside her protest. "How can they reach you?"

She slid a hand into her bag and retrieved a stack of business cards. "Give them one of these. My cell number is on there."

Liam stuffed the banded stack into his pocket. "Now that we have that business out of the way, we can get down to the nitty-gritty."

Josie lifted a brow. "The *nitty-gritty*?"

"When are you going to dump Noah Anson so we can have our first date?"

"Give it up, Gallagher." Warm, familiar lips brushed her cheek. "Josie isn't dumping me."

Liam tipped his bottle of Corona and merely smiled.

"Noah." Josie experienced a rush of pleasure. "I didn't expect to see you here."

"I'm on the city planning commission. We met this afternoon in one of the back conference rooms." His gaze slid between her and Liam. "Am I interrupting?"

For a second, Josie was tempted to let Noah think this was a date. She wasn't sure why she thought that was a good idea. Maybe it was because she had begun to feel so close to him. *Too close.*

The fact that she was so wholly glad to see him scared her. Only in an alternate universe would Dr. Noah Anson be her perfect match. But she respected him—and herself—too much to lie. "Not at all. I met with Lexi about catering the Valentine's Day dinner at your house, then I ran into Liam."

Noah confiscated an empty chair from a nearby table. "Did you get her to agree?"

"Yes. And Sylvie will be handling the cake."

Liam took a long, slow drink of beer. His gaze shifted between Josie and Noah.

"Am I to deduce from this conversation that you and this guy—" the psychologist jerked his head in Noah's direction "—already have plans for Valentine's Day?"

Josie nodded.

Liam gave an exaggerated sigh. "I don't stand a chance."

"You don't." Noah picked up Josie's hand and brought it to his lips for a kiss. "Not a chance in hell."

The psychologist stayed a few minutes longer, then excused himself to greet an associate, Dr. Peter Allman, who'd just walked through the door.

Josie waited until Liam was out of earshot to speak. "You deliberately gave him the wrong impression."

Appearing unconcerned, Noah lifted his glass of beer and smiled. "We are going to be together on Valentine's Day."

"At a dinner party for my *parents*."

"Still counts." An almost boyish grin flashed.

Josie found it hard to stay irritated. "I didn't expect to see you tonight."

"Obviously. Since you were interviewing my replacement."

"I'm not interested in Liam." The words slipped out before she could stop them.

He leaned closer, his voice a low, sexy rumble. "Tell me more."

The attraction shimmering in the air between them only added to her discomfort.

"Why are we even discussing this?" Josie threw up her hands. "Let's talk about something else."

"Snowshoeing tomorrow. Interested?"

The sudden change in topic gave her whiplash. She blinked. "Why?"

"I don't see any reason we can't partake in an enjoyable physical activity while discussing our next move."

Snowshoeing. How long had it been? Too long, she realized.

Discussing further strategies in the great outdoors would certainly be safer than speaking in a public place where they could be overheard. That held true for Pauline's home, as well. Noah's place was private but that presented its own set of problems. Like the fact that she and Noah couldn't seem to be alone without shedding their clothes.

"Sounds like a plan," she said when the silence lengthened.

Noah lifted the glass of wine he'd brought with him in a mock toast. "It's a date."

It wasn't a date, not in the true sense of the word, but Josie lifted her empty margarita glass and decided to heck with semantics.

She and Noah both knew what was, and what was not, between them. That was all that mattered.

After texting Josie early the next morning to confirm she had her own set of snowshoes, Noah arrived at his grandmother's house promptly at nine. He made short work of stowing Josie's gear in the back of his SUV.

He planned for them to snowshoe along the Moose-Wilson Road, a stretch of roadway closed in the winter to cars. The trail was an easy six-mile round trip.

Once they reached the trailhead in Grand Teton National Park, he and Josie quickly clamped in then started out, keeping parallel to the ski trail. The day couldn't have been more perfect, with a vivid blue sky and the air crisp, but not particularly cold.

Noah had been on the trail a couple of times since moving to Jackson Hole. He'd enjoyed the activity, the solitude and the breathtaking views.

Today, all he could see was Josie, her cheeks flushed and her eyes bright beneath a striped cap with a ridiculous tassel. She'd put on a shimmery lip gloss before getting out of the Land Rover, saying something about UV protection.

He was the one who needed some protection—from her and those tempting red lips.

Pulling his gaze away from her mouth, he focused on the ease with which she handled her poles. "You've got good form."

Not to mention an incredibly appealing mouth.

Concentrate, Anson, concentrate.

"I didn't realize you were so athletic," he added, his gaze still on her lips.

"I'm glad you brought that up." Her gaze locked with his. "That's actually what I wanted to discuss."

"Go ahead. Tell me what a good athlete you are." He

exhaled a melodramatic breath. "I'll try not to consider it bragging."

She burst into laughter. The sound was so infectious Noah found himself laughing with her.

"That's not it at all." Though her eyes still danced, her expression sobered. "This is about seeing the good, no matter how small or insignificant."

Overhead a bird cawed, flapping jet-black wings then soaring across the azure sky.

Noah decided he must have looked as confused as he felt because she continued without waiting for him to respond.

"Remember the other night when you mentioned Daffodil's skill with watercolors?"

"I remember."

"Just thinking about all that my father is doing for my mother with this party has softened my opinion of him. The compliment you gave Daffodil had her softening toward you." Josie moved steadily through the pristine white snow, her brows now furrowed in thought. "Both are reminders that people have good qualities as well as bad."

He couldn't figure out why she felt the need to cover old ground. "We already discussed that and decided to give compliments."

"That was for them. This would be for us." She paused and stuck her pole in the ground with unnecessary vigor. "I'm making a mess of this."

She might be mucking it up, but he was a smart guy—brilliant, in fact—and he should be able to figure out what she was trying to say. He'd always been good with puzzles once he put his mind to the matter.

"I see where you're going," he said, a moment later. "You're saying we need to make sure to keep our focus on the good in our family members. That way, we won't get as frustrated with the situation."

Relief spread across her face. "Exactly."

Basking in the warmth of her approval, Noah felt as if he'd just successfully resected an inoperable brain tumor.

"It makes sense." He maneuvered around a fallen log in their path. "I need to keep in mind Daffodil's best qualities, past and present."

"Since you brought up your sister, how 'bout we start with her? Off the top of your head, give me five of her qualities that you admire."

Noah grimaced. He wasn't certain he could even come up with two. Though the purpose of this outing had been to strategize, he didn't want to talk about his sister or even think about her. He wanted to enjoy the beautiful day... and Josie's company.

But when Josie shot him one of her glances, he dug for an answer.

"Daffy is kind," Noah said finally. "When she was small, she was always taking in animals and trying to help them. And she's sweet. She rarely gets angry. If she does, it doesn't last."

"Having her stay angry with you must hurt."

"I can't understand it," he admitted. "I was looking out for her welfare by warning her about that loser."

Josie said nothing.

"Daffy still believes I get pleasure in knowing I was right. I've told her a thousand times I wish I'd been wrong. I wish Cruz had been worthy of her."

Hearing the sincerity in his voice made Josie glad she was helping him. Daffy had a lot to lose if she clung to her stubborn pride. Granted, the neurosurgeon could be arrogant, but in their weeks together, Josie had discovered that beneath all the testosterone and swagger was a decent man. A man who'd stand beside a woman when she needed him. A man she could lean on when necessary. A man worthy of love.

Under the big Wyoming sky, Josie was forced to admit to herself what she'd been trying so hard to deny.

She *loved* Noah Anson.

The realization terrified her. *Doctor* Noah Anson was everything she shouldn't want or need. How love had happened to grow, she wasn't quite sure. When it had happened, well, she wasn't sure of that, either. She only knew that sometime during the past four weeks, she'd fallen in love.

Now she had to figure out what she was going to do about it. And how she was going to bear it if he left town.

Chapter Fourteen

On their way back from Grand Teton National Park, Noah detoured to downtown Jackson. Not only had discussing ad nauseam what they admired about their family members been Josie's idea, she'd also insisted they needed to give five sincere compliments this week to family members.

As Daffodil was slated to come to Pauline's home for lunch tomorrow, Noah was off the hook for tonight. But, feeling a little wicked, he'd told Josie there was no reason *she* couldn't start tonight. The truth was, he had an ulterior motive. He wasn't ready for their time together to end.

Josie worried dropping in on her parents on a Saturday afternoon might seem suspicious if they didn't have a reason for the stop.

He suggested they bring a cake.

Josie had jumped on the idea. Noah listened to one side of the conversation with the baker. When Josie gave him the thumbs-up, Noah bypassed the road to Spring Gulch and took the one into Jackson.

Sylvie's bakery was a small space off Main Street. There was no storefront window, just a small sign with the words *The Mad Batter* in a kooky font on a bright green door.

When they pushed open the door, chimes began to play Def Leppard's "Pour Some Sugar on Me." Noah rolled his eyes but had to admit it fit both the baker and her shop.

The small waiting area was painted a vivid purple and had a minimalist feel, holding only a table that, other than its glossy mahogany shine, bore a distinct resemblance to a picnic table. Chalkboards edged in white lacquered wood decorated an entire wall. Each sported a different saying, all revolving around cake.

Noah's favorite: *Life is short...eat cake first!*

Sylvie hurried into the room from the back, wearing white pants and shirt, her hair pulled up in an oversize baker's hat. "Can I get you something to drink?"

"We're fine. I hope we're not disturbing you," Josie began.

Sylvie waved away the words. "I'm glad you stopped by. I just put a few things in the oven so this is a good time."

Josie inhaled deeply. "It smells wonderful in here."

"Smells are always free." Sylvie smiled.

"We can't stay long," Josie said with a hint of regret. "My parents have plans for later this evening. Noah and I want to pop over before they leave."

"And you want to take a cake to them."

"Yes. It doesn't need to be anything big. I'd like my dad to get a taste and for me to have the opportunity to pump my mother on what flavor of cake she prefers. I think chocolate is her favorite, but I want to be sure."

"I've got a couple you could have. I made these for a bride who asked me to bake smaller versions of several cakes that had captured her interest. She took the one she chose with her to show her mother." Sylvie motioned them to follow her to the back of the shop, an immaculate kitchen area with commercial ovens and shiny stainless counters.

The baker eased two cakes from a large refrigerator and placed them on the counter. "You can have your pick."

One looked like a stack of leather-bound books, while the other was shaped like a tree with the initials of the bride and groom engraved in a heart on the trunk.

Noah appeared stunned.

Josie was in awe. "These are both amazing. I don't know which to pick."

"This one," Sylvie pointed to the tree cake, "is buttercream on the inside. The other is chocolate. If you're thinking that might be your mother's choice, I'd take that one."

"Done." Josie opened her bag and grabbed her wallet. "How much do I owe you?"

"Nothing."

Josie shook her head. "I'm not going to let you give me one of your delicious works of art for nothing."

Out of the corner of her eye, Josie saw Noah continue to stare at the "book" cake with a look of bafflement.

"The bride already paid me. She didn't want to take either of these with her, so the chocolate one is yours."

Reluctantly Josie dropped the wallet into her bag. "Okay, but I'm buying you lunch next week."

"Deal."

She waited beside Noah while Sylvie carefully boxed up the cake. Only once it had been safely stowed in the SUV did Josie call her mother to make sure it would be okay if she and Noah stopped by for a few minutes.

Pleasure rippled through her mother's voice when she said she'd love to see them.

"She sounded excited we were coming over," Josie told Noah on their way to Spring Gulch.

"When was the last time you just stopped by?" Noah asked.

Josie thought for a moment, then flushed. "Not since I came home."

"Why not?" There was no judgment in his tone only curiosity.

"I didn't want to intrude."

"Was that really the reason?"

"What do you mean by that?" she snapped, her voice sharper than she'd intended.

"It seems to me that keeping that distance adds a level of formality to the relationship, a layer of protection."

While she couldn't discount what he was saying, she felt the sting of reproach. "When was the last time you just dropped by to see your sister?"

His jaw tightened. "She'd as likely slam the door in my face as invite me in."

"Maybe," Josie agreed, then amended at Noah's baleful stare, "Probably. It's difficult to make overtures when you're not sure what kind of reception you'll receive."

"As Stephen King wrote in *Pet Sematary*, there is no gain without risk."

"You read Stephen King?" Josie chuckled, her irritation easing. "What other deep, dark secrets are you hiding from me, Dr. Anson?"

"Lots of people enjoy popular fiction," he said stiffly.

She'd embarrassed him. That hadn't been her intent. "I do a lot of reading, too. It just shows you can have more in common with someone than you realize."

He gave a curt nod.

It didn't take long to reach her family's home. Noah insisted on carrying the cake into the house. Not only did he hold the white baker's box, he took her arm to steady her as they navigated the icy driveway.

Before Josie could knock, her mother opened the door, calling over her shoulder. "John, Noah and Josie are here."

Noah and Josie.

Just the way her mother linked their names had a shiver of unease traveling up Josie's spine.

"You brought a gift," her mother added.

"Just a little something I thought you and Dad might enjoy." Josie waited until she stood in the foyer before opening the top of the box. "I, ah, we wanted to thank you for the lovely meal the other night."

While her mother wore tweed pants and a sweater, her father appeared slightly more formal in dark dress pants and a crisp white cotton shirt with tiny blue stripes. Though not elegantly attired by any means, her parents looked much better than she and Noah in their skiwear and hiking boots.

"We can't stay long," Josie blurted, then saw the smile on her mother's face falter.

"I believe what your daughter is trying to say—" Noah placed his palm against Josie's back "—is that we know you have plans for the evening and don't want to take too much of your time."

John's brows furrowed as he gazed into the box. "Is that a stack of books?"

Noah laughed. "It's a cake made to look like a pile of classics. Josie's friend, Sylvie Thorne, made it as a proto-type for a wedding cake."

Dori Campbell's gaze flew to her daughter's face. "A wedding cake?"

Surely her mother couldn't actually think her and Noah…?

"It's for a wedding later this summer. The bride is a

librarian and she wanted Sylvie to make several different designs."

"Books? In the form of a cake?" The confused look on her father's face made Josie smile. Traditional to the end, her dad.

"I'm sure it's delicious." Dori shifted her gaze to Noah. "Would you two stay and have a piece with us? I just made some fresh coffee."

After seeing the hopeful look in her mother's eyes, there was no way Josie could refuse. Plus, if she wanted to know what kind of cake her mother liked, this was her opportunity. And she still had to give five sincere compliments.

"I'd love to stay." She turned to Noah. "Do you have time?"

"Absolutely."

Noah took her hand as they followed her parents into the kitchen.

"This couldn't have worked out better," her father said to Noah. "I've been going through some case notes on a patient I'll be referring to you on Monday. While Dori gets the cake and coffee on the table, let's step into my office and I can review her medical history with you."

Josie felt her temper slowly build. How many times over the years had their dinners, their functions, *her needs* taken second chair to her father's patients?

Before she could speak, Noah's gaze met hers, calm and steady. Something in those deep blue depths had her taking a second breath.

Reframe, she told herself. *Think of a compliment you can give him. Any compliment.*

"Dad."

Her father's gaze shifted to her. Instantly, a wary look filled his eyes. Beside her, Josie felt her mother tense.

Noah's encouraging smile gave her the courage to continue.

"I admire your dedication to your patients. I realize a lot of them are worried and fearful when they come to see you. You always make sure they get the very best care."

Her father simply stared as if waiting for some obscure punch line. Then he smiled. "Thank you, Josie. That's one of the nicest things anyone has said to me in a long time."

"Your father has always had a heart for his patients," her mother confided proudly, when John and Noah stepped into the study. She slipped her arm companionably through her daughter's as they strolled to the kitchen. "Recently I had some medical tests done. Your father insisted on finding a doctor who possessed not only the skills but one who'd see me as a person and not just the woman with heart issues."

Josie paused with her hands on the dessert plates. "Dad mentioned something about the problems you've been having."

She'd tried to keep her voice calm but failed. If she could hear the slight tremor, she knew her mother could, too.

"It's not serious. I have what's called atrial fibrillation." Her mother took silverware along with pretty linen napkins in reddish gold and put them on the table. "It started last summer. I was in the backyard doing some gardening when my pulse became erratic and my blood pressure spiked. I ended up in the emergency room."

Josie's own heart began to pound. While she'd been in Portland teaching yoga and giving massages her mother had been facing a health crisis. "Was that when you were diagnosed?"

"Yes." She motioned for Josie to hold the box while she lifted out the cake. "They put me on medication but I don't like the way it makes me feel. My heart beats regularly, but it pounds even when I'm knitting. Your father hooked me up with a delightful cardiologist who talked to us about balloon cryoablation. I'm scheduled to have the procedure on the sixteenth."

"Are you scared?" Josie blurted out the question before she could stop herself.

"A little, although I've been assured it's a relatively safe procedure." Her mother hesitated. "I know John and Ben will be there, but I'd—I'd like it if you could be there, too."

Josie moved to her mother's side, took her hand. "Of course I'll be there."

"Thank you, sweetie. That means a lot to me."

"I love you, Mom. I know that I don't say it often enough, but I really do love you."

When her mother's arms closed around her, Josie clung to the woman who'd been her anchor for so many years.

"I'm sorry I hurt you by not becoming a doctor," she murmured, her words muffled against her mother's sweater.

Tears slipped down her mother's cheeks, raining droplets of moisture on Josie's hair. "All I ever wanted was for you to be happy."

"I worried you when I took off. I know I did," she said when her mother began to protest. "I'm sorry for it. I just, well, I felt as if I were drowning. I didn't know any other way to save myself."

Her mother stroked her hair with the palm of her hand. "I failed you. I should have seen that you felt pressured. I'm so sorry."

Now they were both crying, but these were tears of love and healing.

"Dori." Her father's worried voice sounded from the doorway. "Is everything okay?"

Her mother gave Josie another hug before stepping back.

She kept her arm around her daughter's waist. "Just having a good cry with my daughter. I needed it."

John's gaze shifted from his wife to Josie then back again. Whatever he saw there must have reassured him because the tense set to his shoulders eased.

When his gaze met Josie's, her father smiled. "It's good to have you home, Princess."

Spending the day with Josie left Noah with more questions than answers. When he finally returned home to a house that suddenly seemed too empty, he opened his laptop. He hoped making a list of the steps he needed to take next to reconcile with his sister would steady him.

Josie was making progress with her family while he and Daffodil were like two boxers circling a ring, both wary and waiting to see what move the other would make.

He keyed in a few possible steps but found his mind wandering. Noah had assumed he and Josie would spend the evening together. He'd suggested she come over and offered to make her dinner. They could watch a movie.

Instead of accepting, she'd pled exhaustion and told him she'd *probably* see him in church tomorrow.

Noah shoved his chair back and stood, then began to pace. Darn right she'd see him in church tomorrow. They were a couple. In Jackson Hole couples attended Sunday services together.

Privately Noah acknowledged they weren't *really* a couple. Still, hadn't he seen more of Josie dressed and undressed in the last month than most people in a serious relationship?

If she'd have come over tonight, they'd likely have ended up in bed together. Instead of dissipating, his need for her continued to grow. That was a worry.

He couldn't help recalling what had happened the last

two times he'd let himself become enamored by a woman. The first time, he'd nearly failed physics. The second, he'd been prepared to choose his top three residency locations based on what would work best for *her*.

Love made him careless, unpredictable, out of control.

That was why he had to keep this fling with Josie on a tight rein. It was ridiculous to think that their relationship stood a chance at lasting.

The smart move would be to slow things down.

Noah glanced at the clock and wondered if it was too late to call Josie and make plans for tomorrow.

Chapter Fifteen

Josie sensed Noah's frustration with the way things were going with his sister, or rather not going. With the party for her mother only a week away and Noah's self-imposed deadline for achieving resolution with his sister looming, they needed an opportunity.

On Tuesday, after a morning meeting with Meg and the other therapists at Body Harmony, Josie decided to grab a quick cup of coffee. The second she walked into Hill of Beans she saw the opportunity she'd been hoping for and seized it. She strolled up to the ethereal blonde waiting in line and asked Daffodil to join her for coffee.

She wasn't confident Noah's sister would agree. Ever since Josie began *dating* Noah, Daffy—who'd been a friend of sorts prior—had turned standoffish. But Daffodil agreed, quite readily in fact.

Josie found an open table by the window. Placing a white chocolate macadamia nut cookie on the plate between them, she settled herself.

She hoped, hoped, hoped this would go well. Noah had been so helpful with her family that she longed to return the favor. Not only that, she knew how good it felt to make peace with the past and move forward. She wanted the same for Noah and Daffodil.

"How are things going with you?" Daffy asked, taking a sip of her chai.

"Busy." Josie warmed her hands around her cup. "Between working for your grandmother, my yoga classes and scouting for locations to set up my massage table, I'm scrambling. Toss in finishing up the final details for my mother's surprise dinner party and, well, let's just say my cup definitely runneth over."

"You make time for my brother."

Josie gazed into those clear blue eyes and sat her cup down without drinking. She felt a spurt of sympathy for the pain reflected back at her. "Your estrangement hurts him as much as it hurts you."

"I doubt that." Daffodil's lips pressed together. "I'm sorry I brought him up. I don't want to talk about Noah. Especially not today."

Breaking off a piece of cookie, Josie forced a casual offhand tone. "What's so special about today?"

"Today would have been my third anniversary." Daffy lifted the cup to her lips and took another long sip. "Instead, I've been divorced for two years."

"Oh, Daffy." The cookie lodged in Josie's throat. She washed it down with a sip of her drink. "I'm so sorry."

"It's best the marriage ended." Daffy carefully placed her cup on the table. Her smile appeared forced. "It bites that Noah ended up being right about Cruz."

"Is the fact that he was right why you won't forgive him?" Asking the direct question was a calculated risk. But Josie had no choice. Subtlety hadn't worked.

Daffy's blue eyes shot to Josie's face. "Who says I can't forgive him?"

"You barely talk to him." Josie kept her tone light. "You don't want to spend time with him."

"Did Noah ask you to come to me?" Blond brows slammed together. "To convince me he's a good guy?"

"Initially, that's what he may have wanted," Josie admitted, unwilling to bend the truth even a smidge. "I know what it feels like to be separated from someone you love. I care about you."

"And about him?" The words sounded more like an accusation rather than a simple question.

"I like Noah." Instead of elaborating, Josie lifted the macchiato to her lips.

Concern filled Daffodil's eyes. "Be careful."

Josie wrapped her hand around the cup. "I'm not sure I understand."

Daffodil hesitated only a second. "My brother can be charming. But he likes to run the show and is convinced he always knows best. Any decisions he makes are based on what's good for him. You go along or he walks."

Josie's insides turned to ice. Sounded entirely too familiar. She broke off another piece of cookie and popped it into her mouth, chewed for a moment. "Is that what happened with you and him?"

"I didn't agree with his assessment of Cruz. And I really didn't appreciate the cold way he conveyed his disapproval. I knew he cared, that was never the point." She looked away, sighed, turned back. "What I can't forgive is that when I didn't do what he wanted, when I married Cruz, he abandoned me."

Josie's fingers tightened around her cup. It wasn't her place to explain Noah's actions to his sister. "How did he do that?"

"He cut off all communication. I didn't hear from him during my marriage. Not that I would have spoken with him anyway." Daffodil blew out a breath. "Now this show of support from him is a little too late."

Josie met Daffodil's gaze. "It's not too late until one of you is dead."

The conversation careened downhill from there. By the time Josie left the coffee shop, she was frustrated and on edge.

She didn't know what to think, who to believe. Could Noah have simply walked away from his sister and stayed away, not because he was giving her space as he claimed but because, as Daffy claimed, she hadn't done what he wanted?

And if he had walked, could Josie hold it against him? She'd done nearly the same thing when she'd walked away from her family. She wondered if her brother held it against her, just as Daffodil held Noah's absence in her life during those years against him.

While Josie had made strides in her relationship with both parents, Ben remained standoffish. Knowing her brother's personality, she had no doubt he harbored some degree of resentment.

Josie strolled by a bakery. When the door swung open, the delicious scent of cinnamon and sugar wafted out into the cool air. The familiar scent made her smile and caused her to pause in front of the shop. Long ago, snickerdoodles had been her brother's favorite.

She could use the cookies as a peace offering of sorts. A tangible reminder of a childhood memory, cookies in front of the fire over a game of Monopoly.

Dropping by the clinic would have the added benefit of allowing her to see Noah. Because of their busy schedules it had been three long days since she'd seen him, six since they'd made love.

Her feelings for him had begun to run deep. When she was around him, she only wanted to be with him more.

Josie told herself that if their relationship was meant to develop into anything meaningful, that would become clear in time.

Daffodil's words added an extra layer of caution. His sister had known Noah her entire life, while Josie had known him only a handful of weeks.

Even as her heart galloped in anticipation of crossing paths with Noah, she kept reminding herself it was Ben she'd come to see. The moment she stepped into the quiet stillness of the clinic, Josie realized this must be a morning reserved for surgeries. Her heart sank. The odds that she'd run into either her brother—or Noah—were small.

She almost turned and walked out when the receptionist noticed her and called out a greeting.

With bakery sack in hand, Josie crossed the plush, richly appointed lobby.

"Hi, Phyllis." Then, because she had an optimistic heart, she added, "Is my brother around?"

"He's in surgery." Noah's voice sounded from behind the receptionist as he came from the outer office into the waiting area.

Josie's body began to thrum the instant she heard his smooth baritone. Her lips seemed determined to lift in a goofy smile. So much for playing it cool.

His gaze shifted from her to the sack. "This is a surprise. Is that for me?"

She lifted the white bakery bag out of reach just before his fingers could close around the top. "These are for Ben."

Curiosity sparked in those brilliant blue eyes. "What did you bring him?"

"Snickerdoodles. They're his favorite. Or used to be," she added, suddenly feeling foolish. Perhaps the cookies hadn't been such a good idea after all.

Understanding filled Noah's eyes. "He'll be sorry he missed you."

She shook her head and shoved the bag at him. "Here. Give these to him."

But Noah only took her arm. "Come with me."

Josie hesitated, though not sure why. Unless it was because she was so wholly glad to see him. Her body felt like it had been asleep for the past three days and was only now awakening. She shrugged and gave in to temptation. Something that was so easy to do around Noah. "Sure. I can spare a few minutes."

As Josie slipped past the front desk, the receptionist stood. "I'm taking my break now, Dr. Anson. I'll lock the front door. Don't forget trauma rounds start in thirty minutes."

"Thanks for the reminder, Phyllis." Noah offered the older woman a smile. "Enjoy your lunch."

The front door closed behind the woman with a click.

"It's like a tomb in here," Josie said as she followed Noah to his office at the far end of the back hall. "Where is everyone?"

"The staff is at lunch." He opened the door to his office and stepped back to let her enter. "I came back to dictate some consults. Ben's in surgery."

Noah lifted the bag from her hand and set it on the large cherrywood desk. "I'll give this to him with your regards."

"Minus a cookie or two?"

He grinned. "Handling fee."

She couldn't resist returning his smile. "What did you want to show me?"

He moved to the door and the lock snicked shut. He turned and pinned her with his gaze. "I missed you."

"I've been busy." She swallowed past the sudden dryness in her throat as her heart began to thump. "We both have."

"I believe in making time for what's important." With a gentle finger he tucked a strand of hair behind her ear. "Which means making time for us."

Josie told herself to step away. Instead she moved to him, winding her arms around his neck.

That seemed all the encouragement he needed. His mouth covered hers in a long kiss that had her toes curling in her boots. He didn't stop there. Noah continued to kiss her until her head spun and she couldn't remember why it had seemed important to keep her distance.

"It feels like forever since you've kissed me," she murmured against his throat when they came up for air.

"Six days. But who's keeping track?" he added and made her laugh.

She loosened his tie and unfastened the top buttons of his dress shirt.

He angled his head but made no move to stop her. "What are you doing?"

"Making it easier to do this." She sank her teeth into his shoulder in a love nip.

"You know what that does to me." His voice turned raspy as he jerked her to him.

Pressed so tightly against him, it was impossible not to notice the erection straining against the front of his dress pants.

When she looked up into his eyes and saw the desire simmering in the deep blue depths, she experienced a surge of feminine power. "Have you ever had sex on a desk?"

"No." He nuzzled her neck. "Have you?"

She arched her head back, allowing him greater access. "No. But, ah, I'm open to it."

"I was thinking of eating lunch at my desk, but—" the tips of his fingers brushed across the front of her shirt, making her nipples strain against her bra "—what you're suggesting sounds more appetizing."

His mouth closed over hers in a scorching kiss that fried every brain cell she possessed and then some. He wasn't the only one starving. Suddenly frantic hands tugged off her coat and, seized with the same urgency, she grappled with the belt around his waistband that didn't seem to want to come off.

In less than two minutes, their clothes lay in scattered piles across the thick gray carpet and his laptop had been relegated to a nearby chair.

When Noah hefted her up on the desk, she laughed breathlessly. "I'm glad you keep a clean desk."

"So am I," he said as his mouth lowered to cover her breast.

Heat shot through her body like lava exploding from a volcano. Unlike previous lovemaking sessions, this one held an urgency, underlain with desperate need.

Josie couldn't get enough of his taste, his touch. When he thrust into her, she cried out. He covered her mouth with his, stifling the sound. Half-crazed himself, he continued to thrust, bringing her—and him—quickly to fulfillment.

With him still blanketing her, she ran her fingers through his hair, tousling the normally meticulously arranged strands.

"I missed you," she said softly. "I missed this."

"Me, too."

When he started to pull away, she wrapped her legs around him, trapping him inside her. He began to grow hard again and she smiled as she kissed his neck.

The rattling of the doorknob barely registered. But the sharp rap on the door had them going still.

"Noah. Are you in there?" Ben's deep voice was laced with annoyance. "You're late for trauma rounds."

Noah cursed and rolled off Josie. "On my way."

He frantically began pulling on clothes.

"Get dressed," he hissed in a low tone, jerking his head in the direction of the door.

Josie scrambled off the desk and quickly donned pants and sweater. She stuffed her underwear into her bag.

By the time Noah opened the door and rushed out—brushing past his colleague—the laptop was back on the desk along with a stack of charts.

She heard Noah say something to Ben about getting caught up and losing track of time, before disappearing from sight.

When Josie stepped to the door, purse slung over her shoulder, her brother's brows slammed together. "What are you doing here?"

It wasn't the friendliest greeting she'd ever received, but what had she expected? At least he sounded more surprised than annoyed.

Josie lifted the bakery sack she'd retrieved on her way to the door and shoved it into his hands. "I brought you some cookies. Enjoy."

His gaze dropped to the bag. He frowned.

"Snickerdoodles, Benedict." She hated that her voice wasn't quite steady.

"Why?"

Josie clenched her hands into fists and resisted the urge to scream. Next time she purchased cookies, she vowed to keep them for herself.

"Because you like them." She spoke to her Mensaeligible brother in a tone usually reserved for small children. "Or you used to, anyway, once upon a time."

When the exterior door jingled, Josie jumped.

As if suddenly conscious of the office staff arriving for the clinic hours, Ben stepped into Noah's office and shut the door behind him. He glanced around the office, his sharp-eyed gaze shifting from Josie's face to the desktop.

She lifted her chin. "Don't knock it until you've tried it."

"Who says I haven't?" His quick grin added credibility to his response, but he quickly sobered. "I don't want you hurt."

Josie shrugged. "Noah and I are just trying to get each other out of our systems."

His gaze narrowed. "Whose idea was that?"

"Does it matter?"

He opened his mouth to say something, then seemed to think better of it. "I guess it's okay, as long as you both agree."

"We do."

"Let's talk about something else." Ben gestured to a pair of leather chairs positioned off to the side. "How've you been?"

How had she been? Seriously, that was what he wanted to discuss?

Trying not to show her trepidation, Josie sat and reminded herself this was what she wanted. She'd come here hoping for some alone time with her brother. Their relationship certainly wasn't going to mend itself. This was her chance to make a chink in that wall between them.

Josie gazed at the brother who was closest to her in age. He'd grown into a handsome man with a commanding presence and a way of looking at her as if he could see right through her.

In his dress pants, shirt, tie and lab coat, he looked every inch the successful doctor. He was also a stranger.

Josie took a deep breath and leaned forward. "I want to apologize to you."

Ben's slate-gray eyes grew hooded, his expression turned guarded.

Josie took a deep breath. "When I left college after my junior year and took off, I felt justified. I—"

"Justified." The earlier control nowhere evident, Benedict jerked upright and shouted the word.

Josie met his angry gaze with a calm she didn't feel. "If you're going to yell, I'll leave."

"Running away." Ben made a sound of disgust. "What a surprise."

Josie didn't shift her gaze from his face. "Even though my friends, my family, my *life* was here, I didn't come home once I'd left school. Do you know why?"

"No. How could I? I've never understood you."

Because you didn't try, she wanted to say, but knew an accusatory response would serve no purpose.

"I was afraid." She dug her nails into her palms when her voice trembled. The old trick worked. When she continued, the words were steady. "I didn't believe I was strong enough to stand up to you and Dad and what you wanted for my life."

"Bull."

Josie met his skeptical gaze. *Say what you feel*, she told herself. *Be honest.*

"Medical school wasn't what I wanted, but I couldn't get any of you to listen."

Ben snorted. "You expect me to believe you ran off because you couldn't stand up for yourself?"

Embarrassment colored her cheeks. She hated being reminded of her past weaknesses. "I wanted so much to please, but I knew if I went along, I'd be miserable. I started seeing a counselor at Student Health. She helped me to see *I* was in charge of my own life, my own destiny."

"Did the *counselor* tell you to run away and worry your family half to death?" The bitter edge to Ben's voice stung like a slap.

"No." Josie stared down at her hands, then lifted her gaze. "She encouraged me to talk with my family and be honest. I tried that at Christmas. You wouldn't listen, none of you."

Ben rose and strode to the window, clasping his hands behind his back. She sensed him looking back. After a minute, he turned.

"I thought it was the stress of school talking." His gaze searched her face. "It appears that was an incorrect assumption."

"When Dad sent me a link for the AMCAS application that spring and you offered to write me a letter of recommendation…" She rubbed her temple. "Well, between all that and my high MCAT scores, I knew I'd be accepted."

Ben unclasped his hands, raised them. "We only wanted what was best for you."

"I never wanted a career in medicine."

"Your leaving came out of the blue, or so it appeared to us," he added when she opened her mouth to protest. "You say you're not coming home, you're going off to find yourself—whatever the heck that means—and we don't hear from you for nine months. When months went by, I feared something bad happened to you."

"I hurt you." Her voice grew thick with emotion. "I'm sorry."

Ben closed his eyes and appeared to fight for control. When they flashed open, Josie saw the regret.

"You had so much potential. I thought, in time, you'd

grow to love medicine as much as I do. I was mistaken. It was never the right course for you."

Their gazes locked and the walls between them began to crumble.

Ben cleared his throat. "What's going on between you and my associate?"

"I love him." Hearing the words surprised her almost as much as they did her brother.

"Seriously?"

"It's crazy, huh?"

"Not crazy." Ben rubbed his chin. "You've been good for him."

"I see the 'but' in your eyes, dear brother. Since we're being totally honest, please don't hold back."

"You're good for him." Ben rubbed his chin again. "I'm not convinced he's right for you."

Chapter Sixteen

A mere two blocks from Noah's office, the hospital rose three stories into the blue sky. Instead of taking the time to get into his car, Noah ran. By the time he sprinted through the automatic front entrance doors, his heart was racing.

How could he have forgotten something so important? The patient being discussed today was his, a young man with multiple injuries from a horrific car accident.

As he reached the door to the conference room, Noah noticed that not only had he left the young man's file, he'd forgotten his laptop. At this point he didn't have time to go back for it. Pushing open the conference door, he stepped inside.

Around the oval table sat several other doctors as well as therapists, social workers and primary care nurses. The purpose of the multidisciplinary meeting was to discuss the care of his patient from when the young man arrived at the ER door via ambulance to his post-hospital rehabilitation needs.

As the doctor who'd operated on the patient and had been most involved with Cory Styles's care, Noah had been charged with leading the conference. His associate, Dr. Mitzi McGregor, sat in the position of command.

"Dr. Anson, I informed the team you were tied up with a patient." The pretty, green-eyed doctor lifted a brow. "Would you like me to continue? Or do you prefer to take over?"

"Please continue, Dr. McGregor." Noah grabbed the life preserver she'd tossed with grateful hands. "There's no need to be repetitive. Everyone's time is valuable."

Mitzi continued with her summation of the treatment that had been rendered to the patient, ending with Noah's recommendation that Cory be transferred at the end of the week to a physical rehabilitation center for continued intensive therapy.

His associate lifted a brow. "Is there anything you'd like to add, Dr. Anson?"

"I have nothing to add." Noah reached up to straighten his tie. He dropped his hands when he realized he wasn't wearing one. Neither was he wearing a suit jacket or even a lab coat. "Excellent summation, Dr. McGregor."

Mitzi smiled and closed her laptop.

The social worker brought up the patient and family's mental state before discussing the insurance coverage. She informed the team there should be a rehabilitation bed available for Cory by the end of the week.

The head of the emergency medicine department, Dr. David Wahl, took the most time. He brought up reports on the screen that analyzed the care Cory had received on arrival. David offered suggestions for improvement and informed the group of changes already made in protocol.

By the time the conference ended, Noah's nerves were strung tight. How could he have let things get so out of control? For God's sake, he'd had sex on his desk that made him late for an important meeting.

He was a doctor. He had responsibilities. But when Josie batted those long lashes at him, he forgot everything else.

Such a loss of control could not happen again. It *would* not happen again. He'd dodged a bullet. The professional reputation he'd worked so hard to build remained intact. Mitzi had covered for him and no one was the wiser.

He caught up with his colleague down the hall and fell into step beside her. "Thanks for filling in."

"No problem. I came to report on his orthopedic needs. When you didn't show I assumed something had come up and took charge."

Noah liked Mitzi. He liked her husband, Keenan, as well. Perhaps sometime he and Josie could go out with—

He stopped the thought before it could fully form. It was being with Josie that had nearly derailed his professional reputation this afternoon.

As they left the hospital and drew close to the clinic, Mitzi's hand on his arm stopped him.

He turned and lifted a brow. "Something wrong?"

"Stand right there." Mitzi reached into her stylish purse and pulled out a small purple brush.

Startled, he remained still while she swiped the bristles through his hair. She stepped back and gazed at him with a critical eye. "Much better."

A chill sluiced through his body with lightning speed. He inclined his head.

"Your hair was…a bit disheveled." She waved a dismissive hand in the air, then her gaze turned impish. "Reminded me of Keenan's hair when I've run my fingers through it."

His blood curdled.

"I looked that way during the meeting?" He pushed the question out past frozen lips.

"I don't believe anyone noticed."

"*You* noticed."

Mitzi gave him a wink. "I notice everything."

If *she* noticed, Noah had no doubt that each person around that table had noticed, as well.

He clenched his jaw. He would not put his career at risk for a woman. No matter how much he liked being with her.

Things were going to have to change.

Josie pulled into Noah's driveway and sat there for a long moment. She couldn't recall the last time she'd felt so at peace. Although things weren't back to where they'd once been with Benedict, she and her brother had made great strides in bridging the distance between them.

Today, they'd related to each other as two adults. She wanted this to be the new normal and believed it would be. For the first time true reconciliation was in sight.

And then there was Noah. He'd let her see the fun, spontaneous side of him he usually kept hidden. She believed it was the increasing closeness and the hard-won trust between them that had allowed him to let go of his old inhibitions.

While she knew he wasn't quite ready to voice his feelings for her, it was just a matter of time. When he'd texted her about needing to see her, Josie had replied that she'd come to him. She needed to take a few more measurements for her mother's party. For a second she'd considered adding something naughty that would make him smile when he read it. At the last second she decided to save the naughty stuff for in-person.

She couldn't wait to see him in the privacy of his own

home. Privacy was essential for the pirate-and-wench role-playing she had in mind for this evening.

Josie fairly floated to the front door. She only had to knock once before it opened. Apparently Noah was as eager to see her as she was to see him. Yet, when she lifted her face for the expected kiss, he reached around her and closed the door.

Well, it *was* chilly outside. She slipped off her coat and waited for him to admire the red sweater that hugged her curves. Instead, he motioned her to the sofa.

Josie's heart skipped a beat. Kissing on the sofa sounded good to her. Measuring and party discussions could wait.

She sat and patted the spot next to her.

Noah took a nearby chair.

For the first time she noticed the lines of tension around his mouth, the tight set to his shoulders. "Noah, what's wrong?"

To her shock, he sprang to his feet and began to pace, hands clasped behind his back. "I've been doing a lot of thinking."

Josie laughed. "That can't be good."

He merely stared.

A shiver of unease crept up her spine. "Ah, that was a joke."

"Yes, well." He paused in his pacing. "How was your day?"

"Great. I enjoyed our time together." The blood in her veins that had started to cool warmed at the memory of how close she'd felt to him earlier. She smiled again, remembering the resulting conversation with her brother. "Benedict and I had a nice conversation after you left."

Noah's gaze sharpened. "About?"

"Nothing to do with us," Josie hastened to reassure him.

Was that why he was in this mood? Was he concerned what Benedict thought? "He understood about the desk."

Noah inhaled sharply. "You told him?"

"He guessed." Josie waved a hand. "That doesn't matter. What matters is him and me, we're okay. I believe we're forging a new normal. I think our relationship is going to be stronger than ever."

"I'm happy for you, Josie." His eyes softened. "I know how much you've wanted that."

"It will happen between you and Daffodil." She reached out and grabbed his hand, realizing it was the first physical contact between them since she'd walked through the door. "You and I, we're going to make that happen."

He pulled his hand gently back and her heart skittered. Something was wrong. But she couldn't figure out what that something was or why Noah seemed determined not to touch her.

"We need to talk."

Were there any other four words that had the power to make a woman's insides curl into a knot?

Josie licked suddenly dry lips, forced a light tone. "I thought that's what we've been doing."

"I mean about us."

The tightness in her chest eased slightly. Suddenly, his nervousness made sense. Obviously, he'd realized his feelings for her and was ready to confess his love.

Her feelings had developed quickly. The intense emotion had freaked her out, but she'd come to accept the truth and knew she'd love Noah till the day she died. Noah was more methodical. She could see him having difficulty coming to terms with something so life-altering.

Josie decided to take pity on him and try to make his confession of love as easy as possible.

"I understand how you're feeling." She lowered her

voice and offered him a reassuring smile. "I've felt the same way for a while now."

"Oh." A startled look crossed his face. "Well, that should make this easy."

"That's what I was hoping." Love for him filled her with a warmth and an overwhelming sense of rightness. She almost let the words of love pass her lips. But knowing Noah as she did, she believed it was important for him to go first.

In fact, he seemed almost impatient with the need to get the words out. Once he did, she hoped he would relax and hold her in his arms.

"Tell me." She coupled the words with an encouraging smile.

Something that almost looked like regret crossed his face, but Josie knew that couldn't be right. Why would he regret loving her? Though he'd never said the words, she knew he did. She'd felt it when he'd made love to her this afternoon.

What had happened on the desk hadn't been merely sex. What she and Noah had shared went far beyond pure physical need.

"We need to slow things down. Take a step back."

What? Slow things down? He couldn't be serious. Stunned, Josie could only stare.

Noah blew out a harsh breath and raked a hand through his hair. "It's for the best."

He *was* serious.

The roaring in her ears made it difficult for her to form a coherent thought.

"I'm not sure I understand," she stammered when she finally found her voice.

"We need to stop seeing each other as much." He clasped his hands together then unclasped them almost immediately. "Take time and regroup."

"Why?"

He blinked and gazed at her as if she'd spoken in a foreign tongue.

"It's a fair question since you're cutting me loose." She waited for a second, hoping he'd deny it. Hoping she'd gotten it wrong.

This time it was he who was silent.

"I have a right to know why."

"I didn't say I was cutting you loose."

"So you want to keep me on the hook but you call the shots."

For the first time, he appeared to notice that she was not as calm as her carefully modulated voice suggested.

"I didn't say that." He spoke cautiously, as if picking his way through a mine field. But it was too late. The bomb had already exploded.

"Let me see if I have this straight." She leaned forward, resisting the urge to shout or flee. "You'll decide how often we'll see each other. You'll say when we have sex. Because you know best."

The sarcasm in her voice came through loud and clear. Noah frowned. "I never said—"

"Don't." The word shot from her lips and she jerked to her feet. "I thought I could trust you. I thought we had something special. I was mistaken."

"I never said I knew best," he said, stubbornly focusing on her earlier comment.

She pinned him with her gaze. "Do you think you know best?"

"Yes," he said automatically, then appeared to reconsider. "I mean—"

"Did you ever consider discussing your concerns— whatever they are—with me? Did you ever consider our relationship—"

"We don't have a relationship."

The words, the dismissive tone, sliced her heart. She slowly rose, wondering how she could have given her heart to such a man.

The signs had been there, she realized. She'd foolishly ignored them. No more. "I'm done."

A startled look crossed his face. "Done?"

"With you." Her heart broke with the words but Josie stayed strong and met his gaze. "I'm not the type of woman you want. That's fine. You're not the kind of man I want either."

"Josie." He grabbed her arm. "Don't be so emotional. Don't run away."

She jerked her arm from his grasp but made herself face him once again.

"I'm not emotional. And I'm not running away." She stared long and hard into the face of the man she loved who didn't love her. "I'm walking out."

Chapter Seventeen

Over the next few days Josie ignored every one of Noah's calls and texts. He concluded she was still angry with him.

His only consolation was that her parents' party was still scheduled for Valentine's Day at his house. She wouldn't be able to avoid him that night.

Noah hoped these days apart had given her a chance to reflect on their last conversation. He'd never said he didn't want to see her again, he merely suggested slowing things down. He still thought it was a good idea.

He knew what happened when a man let his emotions control him. Nothing good came from losing control, as evidenced by his close call with the trauma conference.

Of course, he hadn't counted on missing Josie so much. The intensity of his need for her disturbed him. Somehow, without him knowing it, she'd become an integral part of his life. Now she was gone.

Though he felt her absence keenly, he tried to tell himself that this "breather" was for the best. What he felt for her couldn't possibly be love. How could it be? They'd only known each other for six weeks.

The ache in his heart, well, that was because he'd seen the hurt beneath her anger. Hurting her had never been his intention. He would cut off his right hand before he'd deliberately do or say anything that would hurt her.

But it wasn't love he felt.

It couldn't be love.

And if this tight ache filling his chest *was* love, did it change anything? He didn't like feeling so out of control and vulnerable. No, he didn't like it one bit.

Then again, neither did he like being without Josie.

The fact that he'd driven by his grandmother's house today hoping to catch a glimpse of her made him feel foolish. He had no idea what he'd have said if he'd seen her.

His decision to slow things down had been the right one. It was her emotional response to that dictate that was causing all the problems.

No, he'd done what he thought was best for them, and he wasn't about to apologize.

Still, he'd never thought she'd walk out on him.

Wanting to look her best for her parents' Valentine's Day bash, Josie spent extra time on her makeup and hair. While the party was supposed to be relatively casual, this was a special occasion. She chose a red wrap dress with a necklace of boldly colored stones. Before she left her room she slipped on shiny red heels.

As she had to arrive early, she asked Ben and Poppy if they would also come early and help make sure everything was ready. They were happy to oblige.

She breathed a sigh of relief when they pulled up in front of Noah's house right behind her. Though Josie told herself avoiding being alone with Noah wasn't cowardly, she felt like a coward. Since his little speech about taking a step back and slowing things down, she'd made sure to only come over and finish up when she knew he wouldn't be home.

She simply needed more time. Her feelings were open and raw, like an oozing wound. Her love for him made her vulnerable. Tonight she needed to put on her happy face. There was no way she was going to spoil this evening for her parents.

The second she knocked, the door flew open. Noah looked dashing in a dark hand-tailored suit and bold paisley tie. His gaze lingered on her before shifting to her brother and sister-in-law.

Noah shook Ben's hand. "I didn't expect to see you so early."

Like Noah, her brother was dressed in a suit and tie, while Poppy wore a hunter-green sweater dress the same shade as her eyes. In deference to her pregnancy and the icy sidewalks, her sister-in-law wore flats.

After taking their coats, Noah escorted them to the back of the house.

"This looks wonderful." Poppy gazed in admiration at the long table Josie had festively covered with a Kate Spade–inspired striped black-and-white cloth. Napkins of watermelon pink had been fashioned into bows with striped bands matching the tablecloth.

Pink candle tapers in crystal holders added a touch of elegance to the ambiance as did the bouquets of tulips in crystal bowls. Rose petals in various shades of pink were artfully scattered across the tabletop.

"Very nice," Ben agreed. "My mom is going to love this."

"Josie deserves the credit." Noah's gaze remained fixed

on her face. "She handled the arrangements and the decorations. I only provided the space."

Poppy patted her on the back. "Fabulous job, Josie. I wish I could have been more help. I hate that you had to do so much of this on your own."

"Noah was actually more involved than he's letting on." *Give credit where credit is due*, Josie told herself. Noah had been a big help.

"That's the wonderful thing about effective partnerships." Ben glanced at his wife. "You complement each other."

"That's often true." Josie offered a bright smile, avoiding Noah's eyes. "I should see how Lexi is coming with the meal."

Noah fell into step beside her on her way to the kitchen while her brother and his wife followed behind. "Your mother doesn't suspect a thing."

Josie slowed her steps. "How can you be certain?"

"Your father told me she's excited to come to *our* party."

The emphasis didn't escape her. "*Our* party?"

"That's how your father sold it. That you and I were having a small Valentine's Day party at my house and wanted them to attend."

"Great," Josie muttered. "One more lie."

Her irritation wasn't fair. She'd mentioned their "relationship" as a selling point for having the party here.

Noah paused and looked as if there was something he wanted to say.

Poppy's brows pulled together as if she found herself facing a particularly difficult puzzle she couldn't solve.

"Why is it a lie? Noah is hosting the event in his home and you two are together." Poppy smiled at her husband then focused back on Josie. "Ben told me about your... private consultation...in Noah's office."

Josie felt heat rise up her neck to flood her cheeks. Though the sex had been fabulous, it had been the thought that Noah had changed, had finally let himself embrace the moment that had been so sweet and memorable. Just another lie she'd told herself.

Josie closed her eyes for a second and let out a long breath. When she opened them and saw that she wasn't the only one blushing. Poppy's cheeks were bright pink.

"Until Ben told me that, I was skeptical that the two of you were really together."

Josie took a deep breath. She and Noah might have to pretend for her parents, at least for one more night, but Ben and Poppy deserved the truth.

Before she could speak, she heard Lexi's voice calling to her from the kitchen.

"Josie, when you have a second, come see me please. I have a question."

"Duty calls." Josie's tight smile didn't come close to reaching her eyes. For the first time she fully focused on Noah's gaze. "You explain."

She'd barely stepped away when Ben pinned Noah with his gaze.

"Explain what?" The accusation in his tone had Noah's spine stiffening.

"A slight ripple." Noah had to admit he was surprised by Ben's brotherly concern. He waved a dismissive hand. "Nothing that can't—won't—be fixed with time. Things were moving too fast. Josie took exception to my suggestion we slow things down."

Poppy and Ben exchanged a glance.

"Suggested?" Poppy appeared to be hiding a smile. "Or did you pull a Benedict Campbell and tell her how it was going to be."

"Same thing," Noah insisted.

Ben chuckled and shook his head. "Man, do you have a lot to learn about women."

"Benedict is an expert, Noah." Despite the hint of sarcasm in her voice, Poppy's eyes were warm when her gaze landed on her husband. "Such an expert it only took him nine months to convince me to marry him. And I was carrying his baby."

"You wanted me," Ben said with familiar arrogance. "You just didn't know it at the time."

Poppy laughed, cupped his face with her hand and kissed him gently on the mouth. "True. I'm going to leave you two gentlemen and see if I can be of help in the kitchen. After all, that's why I came early."

"You came early to act as a buffer between Josie and me," Noah said pointedly.

"I see that now." Poppy's eyes held a tinge of sadness. "I didn't realize that until we got here."

Ben fixed his gaze on Noah. "A buffer wouldn't have been necessary if you'd treated my sister well."

"Look who's talking." Noah's jaw set in a hard angle. "Last week you and Josie could barely stand being in the same room together."

"Boys." Poppy actually clapped her hands. "We've got guests arriving soon. I suggest you get busy and not waste time in useless bickering."

After delivering the insulting words, Poppy sailed away, leaving the two men slack-jawed.

"We weren't *bickering*." Even the word was offensive on Noah's tongue.

"Absolutely not," Ben agreed. "Men don't bicker."

For a moment they stood in righteous silence. Then Noah strode to the window overlooking his backyard. The area had received a couple more inches of snow last night so the yard was a pristine blanket of white under the lights.

Set against the backdrop of a brilliant blue sky, the scenery left him as cold as his insides. "You believe I made a mistake."

It may have been a statement, but Noah expected an answer.

"What exactly did you say to her?"

Noah wasn't sure if Ben was stalling for time or if he truly believed details would make a difference in how he responded.

"I told Josie things between us were moving too fast. I thought it best to slow down a bit." The frustration Noah had been holding inside bubbled up and spilled out. "By God, Ben, I was late to trauma rounds. I showed up with my hair a mess. I wasn't even wearing a tie or jacket."

Even though Ben laughed, a sympathetic look crossed his face. "Last time I chaired rounds, I showed up with a smear of grape jelly on my cheek courtesy of my son. Things happen when you have a life outside of medicine."

"Not to me." Noah lifted his chin, daring his colleague to disagree. "I give my patients the best care."

"We give patients the best care by being skilled, knowledgeable and caring," Ben said pointedly. "There is more to the practice of medicine than technique. We need a well-balanced life to have the energy to keep at this day after day, year after year."

Noah gave a grudging nod. "I still don't understand why she reacted so strongly to my suggestion."

"Was it a suggestion or a directive?"

"I'd made my decision."

The statement seemed to tell Ben all he needed to know.

"When you have a patient in your office, do you tell them what you're going to do? Or do you give them options, listen to what they have to say, see what route they prefer to take?"

"I give them options, of course." Noah couldn't hide his indignation. "After I advise them of the facts and my recommendation."

"Do you listen to what they have to say?"

"Certainly."

"Is that what you did with my sister?"

Noah saw the direction Ben was headed. "I didn't have the chance. She walked out."

Even as he voiced the excuse, Noah experienced a stab of guilt. There had been time before Josie left for him to ask for her thoughts on the matter, to get her input.

"She may have thought you wouldn't listen. That's not solely your fault. We—my father, brothers and me—never listened to her. She was the baby and the only girl and we felt we knew what was best for her. It's made her overly sensitive. She probably thought there was no point in a discussion. You'd only try to convince her that she was wrong."

And that, Noah thought, was just what he'd have done. He recalled everything Josie had told him about her childhood, those days at college. Then her guidance on how to listen to Daffy. "Actually, she didn't leave immediately. She tried to discuss the situation with me."

"Which shows she trusts you to do the right thing."

Noah gave a humorless laugh. "Hardly."

Instead of immediately responding, Ben turned and walked away, motioning for Noah to follow.

Noah wasn't certain if Ben didn't want to be roped into helping in the kitchen or because he didn't want to take the chance of being overheard or because he was done discussing the matter.

"Think about it," Ben said when they reached the family room. "Josie told you she didn't agree with your *suggestion*."

If he hadn't felt so stressed, if this wasn't so danged important, Ben's emphasis on the word might have made him smile.

"She made that abundantly clear." Noah rolled his shoulders in an attempt to ease the tension.

"Which means she loves you."

Noah frowned. "How do you figure?"

Ben spread his hands out. "If she didn't love you, if she didn't care, she'd have simply walked away."

The words rang true.

Noah raked his hand through his hair. "I really mucked things up."

"Trust me." Ben clapped a hand on Noah's back. "I made my share of mistakes with Poppy. All's well that ends well, is my motto."

The problem was, Noah wasn't certain this was going to end well. He could handle Josie's anger but it was the cool disinterest in her eyes that made him wonder if he'd irrevocably damaged their relationship.

If he had, that was on him…all on him. For now, he had to figure out what he was going to do about the situation.

Chapter Eighteen

Dori Campbell cried when she realized the party was for her. Then she wrapped her arms around her husband and gave him a kiss that put all of the ones Josie and Noah had exchanged to shame.

Noah.

No matter where she was in the house, she felt his gaze on her. It was a small group so Josie found it impossible to escape him. Other than her immediate family, including her brothers and their spouses, the guest list had been limited to Mitzi and Keenan, Frank and Kathy Reynolds, her parents' oldest and dearest friends, and, of course, her and Noah.

For her parents' sake, all through dinner Josie kept a smile on her face. It wasn't that hard. Everyone in attendance was in high spirits.

It would have been perfect…if Noah hadn't been seated next to her at the dinner table. If he hadn't been around every corner she turned.

Although Lexi had done the catering, once the dinner was served she'd taken off to spend the evening with her own Valentine. That meant it was up to Josie and Poppy to clear the table after everyone had eaten.

Ben and Noah insisted on helping. That made retreating to the kitchen in order to regroup impossible. Though she had to admit she was grateful for the assistance.

Still, watching Poppy and Ben laugh and tease each other while loading the dishwasher was like a knife to the heart. Her brother had certainly mellowed since he'd married the social worker. In fact, Josie scarcely recognized the solicitous husband as the arrogant young doctor he'd been when she'd taken off for Oregon.

Sometimes, there really were happy endings.

Josie straightened. "Time for cake and champagne."

"I'm going to make sure that everyone's champagne glasses are full for the toast." Ben grinned. "Dad has been working all week on it."

"I hope it's better than the ones he used to give at Christmas," Josie murmured, feeling a stab of concern.

"You mean the ones that were more like lectures?" Ben chuckled. "Anything he says tonight has to be an improvement."

"He loves your mother," Noah said quietly. "Some guys aren't goods with words. They screw up. But that doesn't mean the love isn't there. Love should count for something."

But Ben had already left the room.

Poppy's gaze shifted between Josie and Noah before she hurried from the room after her husband.

"Josie," Noah began, "about the other day. I—"

"Josie," her mother called out, a joyful lilt to her voice. "Your and Noah's presence is requested in the living room."

"Showtime." Josie took a breath and plastered a smile on her lips.

Noah reached over and grabbed her hand as they entered the living room. She almost pulled away until she saw the soft look in her mother's eyes. What would it hurt to pretend a little while longer?

"I didn't mean what I said," Noah said, then qualified. "Not really. I mean, not entirely."

"Tonight is about my mother," Josie warned, her whisper soft but firm. "Not us."

"Understood."

Still, he remained beside her, watched as her father stood, took his wife's hand in his.

"Fifty years ago today, I first told this lovely lady—she was but a girl back then—that I loved her. I was fourteen, but when I gave her a heart necklace and told her I'd love her forever, it was a promise I meant to keep." John gazed into his wife's eyes and Josie's heart melted. "Now, fifty years, three sons and a daughter later, she's still the most beautiful woman in the world to me. For as long as I can remember I wanted to be a physician. I love my chosen career, but if I had to choose between her and the practice of medicine, I'd choose her. My life would be empty—" he spoke solely to his wife now "—without you in it."

Tears slipped down her mother's cheeks. Her eyes shone with love.

John shifted his gaze to those in attendance. "Thank you for joining with us to celebrate this special day, for your good wishes and kind thoughts. Now I ask you to raise your glasses as I say to my sweetheart, to my one and only, here's to another fifty."

Everyone cheered then sighed when he pulled his wife close and simply held her tenderly.

Tears sprang to Josie's eyes as she thought of the procedure scheduled in two days.

Noah squeezed her hand. "She'll come through it fine."

She accepted the comfort but as soon as her father sat down, Josie moved to the cake covered with a silver dome.

"When I asked Dad what kind of cake we should get, he confirmed chocolate was Mom's favorite. He also reminded me she liked nothing more than a new pair of shoes." With Poppy's assistance, Josie removed the cover to reveal Sylvie's masterpiece.

The cake was even more beautiful than it had been in the picture. Pale pink frosting covered the entire cake and was decorated with alternating hot-pink and black strips of fondant with shiny little black bows made out of sugar. But the piece de resistance was a gorgeous black stiletto resting on the top of the cake.

A collective *ahh* rose from the group.

Her brother, the event photographer, snapped more pictures.

"It's perfect." Dori turned to her husband and bestowed a watery smile. "This is the best Valentine's Day ever."

"That's not all." John gently placed his hands on his wife's shoulders and turned her back to the cake. "Look inside the shoe."

Dori tilted her head. "The shoe?"

John gave her an encouraging smile.

Her mother stepped to the cake. Being careful not to smudge the beautiful frosting, Dori reached inside the shoe and pulled out a necklace. The sterling silver heart pendant was laden with diamonds. The tears came in earnest now. But the glow on her face confirmed these were happy tears.

The rest of the evening passed in a blur for Josie. She made sure not to be alone with Noah. She knew he wanted to talk but her emotions were already stretched too thin.

After everything was put away, Josie walked out the door with Poppy and Ben.

She felt Noah's gaze on her all the way to her car.

"You need to deal with it," Ben told her.

"I don't know what you mean."

Ben snorted. "You know very well what I mean. Talk to him. Cut him loose or reel him in. It's simple."

"Benedict." Poppy's voice held a warning. "Your sister's love life is none of your concern."

"Of course it is," he said indignantly.

Poppy rolled her eyes.

"I'm not telling her what to do, just…suggesting."

"I'm not dealing with him or anything else until after the procedure," Josie said. "Right now, our mother is my priority."

The next day between his morning hospital rounds and afternoon clinic hours, Noah stopped by his grandmother's house. Josie worked for Pauline every Monday and he hoped to catch her at home.

He knocked, but when no one answered, he used his key and stepped inside. He followed the sounds to the kitchen.

Daffodil sat at the table watching television and eating a salad.

When she didn't look his way, he explained he was on his way to the clinic but had hoped to catch a quick lunch with Josie.

"She has the day off." Daffodil spoke without shifting her gaze from the screen.

"Is she upstairs?" Noah asked.

"Josie is spending the day with her mother." Daffodil took a sip of soda, still without giving him the courtesy of her full attention. "I don't know why you're here. I heard you two aren't seeing each other anymore."

The words drew blood, which he knew from her smug tone was her intention.

"We may have hit a bump in the road. I'll make it right."

Her gaze remained on the television. "Good luck with that."

It seemed his cue to leave. Not just his grandmother's house, but Jackson Hole.

It struck him he didn't want to leave. He wanted to stay, to build a life here surrounded by friends and family, a family that would include Josie and his sister.

"I didn't mean to hurt you when I told you my feelings about Cruz, when I warned you not to marry him." Noah shoved his hands into his pockets and rocked back on his heels.

She turned accusing eyes on him. "You caused a scene at my wedding. I was humiliated."

"I only wanted to protect you. I realize now I could have handled the situation differently. I'm sorry."

Daffodil continued to stare at the television for such a long time he wondered if she'd even heard him. Until he saw the tears welling in her eyes.

"Don't cry, Daff." Instinct had him moving to her side. "I never could stand to see you cry."

She swiveled in her chair and pinned him with those big blue eyes. "Go away, Noah. For the record, I don't forgive you. If Josie is smart, she won't either."

By the time the first hour of her mother's surgery had passed, Josie's nerves were strung as tightly as a piano wire. Her father had taken the day off and Ben had rescheduled his surgeries until the afternoon.

The three of them sat together in the spacious surgical waiting room. Poppy had come down with a cold, so had opted to stay at home and keep in touch by cell phone.

She knew her father and Ben must find it odd to be sitting on this side of the operating room. Normally, they were mending and fixing, then coming to find the families in this waiting area with its soothing lavender walls and soft leather chairs. There were several televisions mounted on the wall with the sound muted.

A thin woman with pure white hair sat at the desk. She'd asked Josie for her name and cell phone number when she arrived. Josie had been instructed to keep "Gladys" informed if she had to leave before her mother's surgery was completed.

Gladys had kind eyes, a calm demeanor and a sweet smile. The salmon-colored smock she wore identified her as a hospital volunteer.

Josie glanced around the quiet room. Except for a middle-aged couple, the three of them were the only ones there.

"Where is everyone?" she asked her father. "I thought Tuesday was a big surgical day."

"It varies for the other specialties. Dad and I rescheduled our patients," Ben informed her. "Mitzi and Noah are the only two from our practice operating this morning."

Noah.

She nodded, not trusting herself to speak.

"Josie and I will get you some coffee," Ben announced to his father, pulling to his feet.

John looked as perplexed as Josie felt. "I've had enough this morning."

"You can toss it if you decide you don't want it." Ben's jaw jutted forward in that bulldog look Josie remembered from their childhood. He motioned for Josie to get up.

She did, only because she'd barely got there and she was already feeling antsy. With at least another three hours to go, they were in for a long wait.

When they reached the coffee station, Josie programmed a cappuccino while Ben poured himself and their father a cup of coffee.

But when she turned to return to her seat, Ben touched her arm. "There's something I want to say to you."

"Really, Ben? You want to get into it now?" She lifted the cup with fingers that trembled.

"This isn't anything bad." He placed a warm hand on her shoulder. "But it's been gnawing at me so I need to get it off my chest."

Josie braced herself. "Tell me."

"Watch yourself with Noah. Don't rush into anything."

She studied her brother, noting his serious expression and the concern reflected in his eyes. She could tell him that she and Noah wouldn't be seeing each other anymore, but that would likely prompt questions she didn't feel like answering at the moment.

She took a sip of cappuccino, more as a way to buy her a few seconds than out of any thirst. "I thought you liked him."

"He's an excellent physician and surgeon."

Coming from her brother, the words were high praise. "Then what's the problem?"

"I'm not sure Noah is right for you." Ben shifted from one foot to the other, appearing slightly embarrassed. "When a man is in love, that woman is the most important person in his world. I want you to be the most important person in the world to him. I'm not sure you are."

Josie experienced a tightening in her throat at the concern in his voice. She gave her brother a reassuring smile. "You don't have to worry about me. I won't settle for less than I deserve, Ben."

"Good." He spoke almost brusquely. "We should get back."

"You were worried about me."

Ben glanced at the ceiling, then across the room where their father sat, staring at them with a quizzical expression.

"I love you, too." Josie sat down her cup and gave him a quick hug before he could arm himself with the coffee.

"Be careful."

Another hour passed and each time the doors slid open from the surgical area, they looked up. Mitzi came out to speak with the middle-aged couple, then stopped briefly to chat before hurrying back to prepare for her next procedure.

"If Noah is doing surgery," Josie asked in a casual tone. "Where is that patient's family?"

"Sometimes the family can't get off work, or there is no family or friends." Her father stared down into the cup then back at his daughter. "I know it reassured your mother to know we'd be here waiting."

Josie squeezed his arm. "I wouldn't miss it."

She wasn't just here for her mother, she realized. She was here for her father and brother. And they were here for her. Because they were her family. And they loved her.

Suddenly overcome with emotion, Josie laid her head against her father's shoulder. He stroked her hair. She closed her eyes.

"I didn't expect to see you out here," she heard her brother say.

"I wanted to touch base. See how everything is going."

Josie opened her eyes and jerked upright at the familiar voice.

"The procedure is just getting started," John said.

Noah stood before her father dressed in blue scrubs and cap. The color emphasized the cerulean blue of his eyes.

Her heart turned into a painful mass in her chest.

His gaze lingered on her. "How are you holding up?"

"I'm hanging in there." Her smile felt stiff. "Thanks for asking."

"It's difficult to wait while someone you love is in surgery." Noah took a step forward but must have seen the warning look in her eyes and stopped. "If there's anything I can do, please—"

"I'm fine. We're fine," she said, imploring him with her eyes to go and leave her alone.

"I've got another procedure scheduled." She expected him to turn, but instead he rested a hand on her shoulder. "I'm serious. Anything at all."

Her bottom lip quivered but she steadied it. "Thank you, Noah."

After speaking for another minute with her father and brother, Noah disappeared through the sliding doors.

"He sure holds you in high regard," her father said, turning to her.

Josie lifted a hand, gave a dismissive wave. "He came by for you."

John shook his head. "No," he said, his voice firm. "He came by for you."

Josie cast her gaze on her brother for support.

A thoughtful look fell over Ben's handsome features. "I believe I may have misjudged the situation."

Chapter Nineteen

Josie stayed at the hospital until her mother was out of recovery and transferred to a medical floor. The procedure had been a success and normal heart rhythm had been restored.

After making sure their mother was stable, Ben had left to scrub for surgery. Now it was only her father and her in the room. And, of course, the nurse who kept coming in to check on her patient.

"Are you sure you don't need me to hang around?" She slanted a glance at her mother, lying flat on her back with her eyes closed. Her skin looked pale and waxy against the whiteness of the sheets.

Her father gave her hand a reassuring squeeze. "There's nothing more to be done. I imagine she'll spend the rest of the evening resting."

"I don't want her to be alone."

"I'll stay with her." The lines around his eyes seemed to have deepened and his features held a weariness that tugged at her heartstrings. His gaze met hers. "It means a lot to her—and to me—that you were here."

"I love her," Josie said simply, staring up into his tired eyes. "And I love you, Dad."

Unexpected tears filled her eyes. She hadn't slept well, she'd been too worried about her mom and the procedure. And, she had to admit, seeing Noah had thrown her off balance. He'd been so kind, so solicitous. She'd gotten the feeling he truly cared.

Suddenly, it was just all too much. Despite her best efforts to contain them, tears spilled from her lids.

"Ah, honey." Her father pulled her to him and held her close, the way he had when she'd been a scared little girl.

She'd always felt safe in his strong arms, as if nothing—and no one—could ever hurt her.

"It will all be okay," he murmured in a deep, soothing tone that was just short of a croon. "I promise."

"I'm sorry for everything, Daddy." She closed her eyes and just clung to him. "I never meant to hurt you by running away."

He patted her back. "I should have listened to you. You told me what you wanted and I didn't listen. I'm sorry for that."

His chin dropped to rest on top of her head. "Your mother and I, we never stopped loving you."

"Even if Noah and I aren't together?" She wasn't certain what made her bring up Noah. Unless it was the fact that seeing him today had the longing for what might have been surging forth.

Her father stepped back and held her out at arms' length, his gaze scanning her face. "I like Noah. He's a fine doctor, a good man. But your relationship—or lack of relationship—with him has nothing to do with my feelings for you."

Relief washed through Josie like a fresh summer rain.

"Since we're talking about this, I'm proud of what you've done with your life." His tone brooked no argument. "I'm very glad you're home."

"I'm happy to be back." Before she left the room, promising to return later, she gave her father a swift, hard hug.

"It will all be okay, Princess." Her father's confident tone, with its touch of arrogance, reminded her of Noah. "It will all be okay."

Josie only wished she could be so confident.

Josie returned home and heard Daffodil and Pauline talking in loud voices in the parlor. She tried to slip by and up the stairs to her room without being noticed, but she wasn't fast enough.

"Josie, how's your mother?"

Though she wanted nothing more than to crawl into bed, close her eyes and try to make sense of all the emotions swirling through her, she knew Pauline was genuinely concerned.

Bypassing the stairway, she turned into the parlor. Both women stood by the fireplace. Pauline, stylishly attired in dove-gray pants and a dark gray sweater, looked serene while Daffodil, dressed in skinny jeans and an oversize sweater, looked anything but serene, with red-rimmed eyes and an anxious expression.

Josie vowed to give her report quickly then head upstairs. Between her mother's surgery and Noah's unexpected appearance, her drama basket was filled to overflowing.

"The procedure went extremely well." Josie lifted her lips in a satisfied smile. "She's out of recovery and resting comfortably in a private room. My dad is with her now. I was going to grab a few minutes rest, then head back to the hospital."

"Wonderful news." Pauline actually clapped her hands, her smile broad.

"I'm happy it went well," Daffodil said in a subdued tone.

As much as Josie wanted to ignore Daffodil's obvious distress, she couldn't. She took a step toward the pretty blonde. "Is everything okay?"

"Yes." Daffodil blinked rapidly. "Excuse me a second. I—I need to do something."

She rushed from the room, leaving Josie to gape after her in astonishment.

Josie turned back to Pauline. "What's wrong?"

"Cruz called and got her all stirred up." Pauline sighed heavily. "I'm just glad Noah isn't around. I fear she'd take out all her hurt and anger on him."

"Not around?"

"He flew to Chicago today."

Josie's heart slammed against her chest, making breathing suddenly difficult. *Chicago. Where his friend Edward Jamison lived.* "I just saw him at the hospital. He stopped by during the surgery. He didn't mention anything about leaving town."

She was grateful her voice didn't betray any of her inner turmoil. Or reflect the fear that suddenly gripped her.

"I believe it was a last-minute kind of thing." Pauline brought a finger to her lips. "I think he bought the ticket only a couple days ago."

"Do you know why he went there?"

Pauline shook her head. "He has a friend there. He mentioned the trip in passing. We got interrupted and I never did get around to asking."

As if realizing Josie was more than a little interested in this trip, Pauline's gaze sharpened. "Do you—"

The ringing of Josie's phone stopped Pauline's words. *Meg Lassiter.*

"I'm sorry." She flashed Pauline an apologetic smile as she headed out of the room. "I need to take this."

Josie spoke with Meg on her way to her room. The call didn't take long. Meg offered her a position at Body Harmony. They set up a time for Josie to come in, meet with the rest of the team and discuss terms and expectations.

Josie's heart pounded against her ribs. Body Harmony was the premiere therapy group in Jackson Hole and her dream place to work. Now she would have a full-time job with benefits and the opportunity to set her own hours.

Which meant she'd be able to continue—and perhaps expand—her yoga classes. Not only that, she'd have time for a social life. She and Noah—

She stopped the thought before it could fully form. She and Noah weren't together anymore. They'd never really been together.

Perhaps it would be best if he moved to Chicago. As hard as it would be for her to watch him go, seeing him every day, knowing he didn't love her, didn't want her, would be difficult to bear.

But he came to see me while my mom was having surgery.

She had to stop wishing and hoping and deal with reality. Noah hadn't come by the waiting room to comfort and support her. He'd come for his practice partners and perhaps because he liked her mother. Hadn't he and Dori bonded over scrapbook pictures and cake?

Josie forced her thoughts from Noah to her good news. She was still reeling that she'd actually gotten the job.

Lexi's recommendation had been a big factor. While she was thinking of it, Josie dialed the social worker.

Minutes later, Josie hung up more confused than ever. Lexi denied having an influence. She said Meg had informed her Josie had wowed them in her interview and that, along with Noah's stellar recommendation, had been enough.

If Lexi's timeline was accurate, Noah had contacted Meg after he'd told Josie he wanted to slow things down, *after* she'd walked out on him.

It didn't make sense. She lifted a hand to her head. None of this was making any sense.

Could her father and brother be right? Did Noah really care?

But if he did, why was he taking the job in Chicago?

When Noah returned to Jackson Hole two days later, he called Josie and asked if she would come over. He said he had something to tell her.

He'd obviously taken the job in Chicago. The coward in her insisted she didn't need closure. But Josie knew that in order to survive losing him she needed to say goodbye and thank him. Not only for his call to Meg Lassiter but for all he'd done for her and her family.

As she drove to his house, she gave herself a pep talk. She'd be gracious and happy for him. She'd wish him well.

Her resolve lasted until he opened the front door, looking sexy as sin in dark pants and a gray sweater. She nearly lost it. Why, oh, why did she have to go and fall in love with him?

It was supposed to be a simple business arrangement but she'd complicated it.

"Hi, Noah." She stepped inside out of the wind. "Welcome back."

He took her coat and cocked his head.

"Your grandmother told me about your trip to Chicago."

"Oh," was all he said.

A fire burned cheerily in the hearth, adding a golden glow to the homey room. She loved this house, the feel of it. If she was being absolutely truthful, she'd secretly thought it would be easy to make this house her home. She could see little dark-haired, blue-eyed children running across the hardwood and a dog, something small and white with a happy smile, toenails clicking as he pranced after them.

She felt Noah's eyes on hers and flushed, before reminding herself he could *not* read her mind. Covering her sudden awkwardness with a smile, she sat in an overstuffed chair and perched on the edge of the cushion. "Did you have a nice talk with your friend?"

Noah took a seat on the sofa, leaned close, resting his forearms on his thighs. "I did."

The pleased look in his eyes had her heart sinking all the way to her toes.

"That's good." Josie kept her tone light. "You mentioned he's an exceptional neurosurgeon, so having him as a partner will be great. I haven't spent a lot of time in Chicago but I'm certain this will be a fabulous career move. I know how important your medical career is to you."

When she stopped to take a breath, Josie realized with sudden horror she'd been babbling. She clamped her mouth shut and tried to remember exactly why she'd come here.

She needed to thank him for the recommendation he'd given Meg. And then, she needed to say goodbye.

Because saying the first would inevitably lead to the second and the end of their conversation, Josie remained silent.

Her gaze lingered on the face that had grown so dear. *I*

love you, she thought with a stab of pain that nearly stole the breath from her lungs, *I will always love you*.

She was attempting to still her rapidly beating heart when he reached over and took her hand.

Her eyes widened, but she didn't pull away. She wanted the connection too badly. This moment would be something she'd remember always, the soft look in his eyes and the tender touch.

"Practicing medicine is important to me." He paused to clear his throat. "But it means nothing without you in my life."

Josie's heart stumbled. She wondered if she was hallucinating. When you wanted something so badly, was it possible to imagine the words you yearned to hear? She hesitated, not about to make a fool of herself by responding to a sentiment that was implied yet not voiced.

"I now understand why you wanted to slow things down between us." Somehow she managed to bring a smile to her lips. "I mean, it only makes sense, what with your upcoming move to Chicago. We'd have to say goodbye soon anyway. I—I sincerely wish you the best."

A startled look crossed his face. "I'm not going anywhere."

"But you said the talk with your friend went well."

"I declined his offer. I met with him in the hopes of selling him on the idea of coming to Jackson Hole. We've been wanting to add another neurosurgeon. Edward is well-qualified for the position."

"You're not leaving town?" Her voice came out on a high-pitched squeak.

When his thumb began to massage her palm, Josie realized he still held her hand. Even as he caressed the sensitive flesh, his gaze remained firmly focused on her face. "I could never leave you."

She didn't dare hope. "You're staying because of your sister, because you haven't yet reconciled."

"I've accepted that Daffodil needs more time." A look of sorrow flitted across his face but was gone in a heartbeat. "I believe Daffy will come around, but in her own time."

She gave a jerky nod. "I believe that, too."

Noah stared into her eyes. "I love you, Josie."

She brought trembling fingers to her lips. "You—you said you wanted to slow things down."

"I meant it at the time. It wasn't anything you'd done, it was me. I wanted you so much, it scared me."

She gave a little laugh. She couldn't help it. Noah Anson frightened? "I don't believe it. Nothing scares you."

"It's true. Not easy to admit. But true. When you walked away, well, it brought me to my knees."

The shaky breath he took told her the effort it took for him to bare his soul. But when she opened her mouth to reassure and soothe, he closed it with a gentle kiss. A kiss filled with promise and love.

He pulled back.

"I love you, Josie Campbell, and I can't bear the thought I may have lost you." His gaze searched hers. "Tell me we can work this out."

She nodded and pushed the words past suddenly dry lips. "We can work this out."

"I don't want to take this slow," he repeated, as if determined to make sure there was no misunderstanding. "I know what I want and she's right here in front of me. You bring such joy into my life. I want to spend the rest of my days bringing the same joy into yours. I want you to be my Valentine, not just on February 14 but every day of the year."

Tears slipped down her cheeks, but Josie could no more

stop them than she could stop the love that swamped her. She
wanted to laugh and sing and dance, all at the same time.

Keeping his gaze firmly fixed on her face, Noah dropped
to one knee beside her, reached into his pocket and pulled
out a velvet jeweler's box. He flipped it open to reveal a
marquis-cut diamond nestled in a platinum setting.

She gasped as the overhead light caught the stone,
shooting brilliant shards of color throughout the room.

"Marry me, Josie. Be my wife, the mother of my children. Be the woman I will honor and cherish and love as
long as I live." Noah didn't wait for an answer. He slipped
the ring on her finger. "Say yes."

"Yes, oh, yes." Josie flung her arms around his neck
and held on for dear life.

She was finally where she belonged, in the arms of the
one man who would love her and who she would love,
forever.

An hour later Josie sat cross-legged across from Noah
on the bed, a bottle of wine and a small, half-eaten red
heart-shaped cake on a plate between them.

After sealing their engagement with some rather enthusiastic lovemaking that put any pirate and wench playacting to shame, Noah had excused himself. When he'd
returned to the bedroom, he'd brought a huge tray containing a bouquet of red roses, along with the wine and cake.

"I love all this." Josie waved a fork in a gesture that en-
compassed the items on the tray.

"I had the candles lit, the flowers on the table and the
wine ready." He gave a rueful smile. "But when I saw you,
sitting in the glow of the firelight, I couldn't wait. I had to
tell you how I feel."

"It's a moment I'll remember and cherish forever." She

leaned forward and kissed him, enjoying the taste of sugar and wine on his lips.

She'd learned the exceptionally fine bottle of red they'd been enjoying had been given to Noah by her father, when Noah had stopped by to ask for his blessing.

The fact that Noah would follow such convention touched Josie's heart. She was certain her conservative father had been thrilled by the gesture of respect.

She glanced at the cake, which had once boasted "Be Mine" in a pink flowery script font across the top. "I can't believe you got The Mad Batter to bake a heart-shaped cake and one with *red* icing. Tradition is hardly Sylvie's forte."

"I specifically asked for that shape and color. I believe she put aside her reservations and made it because of your friendship." His gaze studied hers. "And, perhaps, because she could see it was important to me. I'm a traditional guy. I like the idea of building on customs from generation to generation. I like the idea of being married to you and forming our own traditions in the years to come."

Josie's heart overflowed with love for this man who one day soon would be her husband. She glanced at the diamond sparkling brightly on her left hand. "I want to build a life with you, Noah. I want to have children with you and grow old together."

Moving the tray aside, he tugged her to him, his strong arms closing around her. "You're my perfect match."

"I'm your Valentine." She snuggled close and gave a happy sigh. "And you're mine."

"Forever," he murmured. "And always."

* * * * *

MILLS & BOON®

Cherish™

EXPERIENCE THE ULTIMATE RUSH OF FALLING IN LOVE

0216/23

MILLS & BOON®

Why shop at millsandboon.co.uk?

Each year, thousands of romance readers find their perfect read at millsandboon.co.uk. That's because we're passionate about bringing you the very best romantic fiction. Here are some of the advantages of shopping at www.millsandboon.co.uk:

* **Get new books first**—you'll be able to buy your favourite books one month before they hit the shops

* **Get exclusive discounts**—you'll also be able to buy our specially created monthly collections, with up to 50% off the RRP

* **Find your favourite authors**—latest news, interviews and new releases for all your favourite authors and series on our website, plus ideas for what to try next

* **Join in**—once you've bought your favourite books, don't forget to register with us to rate, review and join in the discussions

Visit **www.millsandboon.co.uk**
for all this and more today!